THE CHERRY VALLEY MIDDLE SCHOOL NEWS

DEAR KNOW-IT-ALL!

★ ★ ★

OLD STORY, NEW TWIST

by RACHEL WISE

Simon Spotlight

New York London Toronto Sydney New Delhi

SIMON SPOTLIGHT
An imprint of Simon & Schuster
Children's Publishing Division
1230 Avenue of the Americas,
New York, New York 10020
Copyright © 2012 by Simon & Schuster,
Inc. All rights reserved, including the
right of reproduction in whole or in
part in any form.
SIMON SPOTLIGHT and colophon are
registered trademarks of
Simon & Schuster, Inc.
Text by Elizabeth Doyle Carey
Designed by Laura L. DiSiena

For information about special discounts
for bulk purchases, please contact
Simon & Schuster Special Sales at
1-866-506-1949 or
business@simonandschuster.com.
Manufactured in the United States of
America 1012 FFG
First Edition 10 9 8 7 6 5 4 3 2 1
ISBN 978-1-4424-5328-9 (pbk)
ISBN 978-1-4424-5385-2 (hc)
ISBN 978-1-4424-5329-6 (eBook)
Library of Congress Control Number
2012947363

Chapter 1

JOURNALIST CAN'T KEEP QUIET, TROUBLE ENSUES!

★ ★ ★

When I am the editor in chief of the *Cherry Valley Voice* next year, I will let people pick their own article topics. I will not assign them whatever boring story I want, just because I can.

The headline of my first issue will say, *Martone Frees Writers from Shackles, Staff Rejoices!*

So there.

In case you can't tell, I am a little annoyed right now at the editor in chief of our school paper. I don't like the article that she and our faculty advisor, Mr. Trigg, have assigned to me for the next issue. And I really don't like the fact that they have separated me from my unofficial writing partner and crush of my life, Michael Lawrence.

I have known Michael Lawrence forever, but I only started loving him last year, and we only began working together this year. He is by far the best-looking boy in the school, and I say this not as an opinion, but as a fact. Lots of other girls think it too, and I can cite my sources, like the good reporter that I am. But I won't, because if there's one thing I don't like to think about, it's other girls and Michael. My best friend (also forever) is Hailey Jones, and she says Michael likes me back. She also has concrete facts and evidence that point to this, but most days I find it a little hard to believe, since nothing has ever come of his so-called liking me.

For instance, Michael insists on calling me "Pasty," a nickname he made up in kindergarten when I tasted the paste in art class. (I was five, I thought it was frosting, blah, blah, blah.) But Hailey says that Michael calling me nicknames means he likes me.

She also points out that he has baked his famous cinnamon buns just for me on more than one occasion. I argue that it could be coincidence, or they might have been leftovers, but she is firm on this point.

Hailey also insists that Michael intentionally stole (rather than "found," as he claimed) my trusty reporter's notebook that I carry everywhere, in order to learn my secrets. Luckily, I had blacked out all the sensitive information in there before it fell into his hands. (A reporter can't be too careful!)

Another thing Michael does is carry granola bars around in case I get hungry. Hailey says that if a boy consistently brings you a snack, it means he is thinking about you. (And not just that he wants to prevent your stomach from rumbling in an interview.)

Anyway, all I know is that if there are this many (and more) reasons why Michael Lawrence supposedly likes me, then why doesn't he ask me out or something?

We get along pretty well, and he likes to tease me (Hailey says this is a good sign too), and we certainly work well together. Or we used to, anyway. Who knows if we will ever work together again?

Here's what happened: At our bi-weekly editorial meeting yesterday after school, where we get together to go over the previous Friday's issue and make plans for the next one, Michael pitched an article about the school district's investments. I perked up, waiting to see if Mr. Trigg (faculty advisor) and Susannah Johnson (editor in chief) would like it enough to assign it to us, since by now it's basically an unwritten rule that Michael and I write together.

Well, they liked it all right, but out of nowhere, Susannah suggested that Michael write it with Austin Carey because his dad works in finance, and Mr. Trigg thought that was a "smashing idea!" (He's British and he always says things like that.) Well, I can tell you one thing I wanted to smash after that meeting, and it wasn't an idea.

Michael was excited that they liked his idea, and then Austin came over and high-fived him and they began brainstorming right away, so I don't even think he was sad we wouldn't be working together. And if that's the case, how can he possibly like me? Humph. He didn't even say good-bye to me when I left the room. Well, Michael can just see if Austin

Carey saves him a seat when he's late for events, or if Austin Carey takes great notes in interviews to back up Michael's supposed steel-trap memory, or if Austin Carey comes up with amazing headlines.

Well, that was how I felt all last night. Just plain mad. Now I'm also disappointed, hurt, frustrated, and sad, and I'm sure more feelings are on the way. Oh, I'm also scared. That's actually the main one. I'm scared that if Michael and I aren't paired together on a story, then we won't see each other at all. Because when we are working together, we usually have lunch together, then we sometimes meet to go over stuff, then we e-mail back and forth. And now, without a reason or excuse to be in contact, I'm not sure he'll ever speak to me again! After all, without a story to work on, I can't exactly ask him to have lunch with me, can I? I might as well put a headline on the front page of the paper that says *Martone Loses Her Mind, Openly Declares Love to Crush.*

Anyway, I will be very busy, so it's not like I'll have time to hang around and pine over my lost love. Susannah gave me a boring assignment for the next issue, and that is part of what makes Michael's assignment so annoying to me. I know on the one hand that I should be glad to have an easy gig this issue, because many of the articles I've worked on lately have taken up a lot of my time. This one won't. But the thing is, my recent assignments have been interesting. This one just isn't.

Here's what I have to do: interview a bunch of eighth graders who are graduating this year and ask them what their happiest memories of Cherry Valley Middle School are, whether they have any regrets, and what advice they would give to other students in the sixth and seventh grades. Fascinating, right? A regular snoozefest if you ask me.

I don't mean to be a bad sport, but come on. This is sixth-grader work, not ace-reporter-probably-next-year's-editor-in-chief-unless-Michael Lawrence-gets-it work. It will take me all of a day. I can probably take a nap at my desk while some boring eighth grader drones on and on at the other end of the phone, and I'll still catch the gist of it. The only hard part is going to be making the article seem interesting.

Meanwhile, I do have quite a lot of mail coming in to my secret, private mailbox. As the *Cherry Valley Voice*'s Dear Know-It-All columnist, I give advice to students who submit letters or e-mails. And it's all anonymous—nobody, and I mean *nobody* other than Mr. Trigg—knows I'm Dear Know-It-All. Not even Hailey.

When Mr. Trigg called me at home at the beginning of the school year, I thought he was firing me from the paper. But it turned out he wanted me to write the advice column. This actually is a top assignment, and for the person who writes it, it usually means you're at least on track to be editor in chief the following year. If you don't make a mess of things, that is.

Well, I've been in a few sticky situations so far this year, but I haven't made a total mess of anything yet. One thing is for sure: The volume of letters I get has been increasing. And that's a good thing, because it gives me more options to choose from when I pick what I'll answer each week. Many of the questions are pretty dumb, like "How do I pass math?" (Um, study?) But some are juicy and a few are even really sad. Sometimes I need Mr. Trigg's help in dealing with some of the situations, and he's been really great so far. I do like him a lot, even if he has separated me from my crush like a wicked king in a fairy tale.

After morning classes today, I stormed off to the cafeteria to find Hailey so I could rant and rave. Luckily, I spotted her right away, on the food line, looking for me. I got a tray and skipped the line in favor of the special table where they offer an organic option every day. Today it was lentil soup with a whole-grain roll. Pretty tasty, and only a dollar!

I looked around for a place to sit, and as I glanced around the room, I spied Michael Lawrence and Austin Carey sitting at a table in the corner, chatting away. My blood began to boil all over again. That should be *me* sitting there with Michael, not Austin! Michael is *my* writing partner, not his! I realized I was staring, and I quickly looked away, pretending I hadn't seen them. I hoped Michael hadn't noticed me looking. I knew one thing, though: I was *not* going to act like I cared that we had been separated. After all, hadn't Michael had a chance to say, *I'm sorry, but as much as I'd like to work with Austin, I'd love to work with Sam again?*

Humph!

"Ready, Sammy?" said Hailey, suddenly at my side. Her tray was loaded down with her usual odd food choices—rice with butter, chocolate pudding, chocolate milk, and saltines.

"Just as long as we're sitting far away from Michael," I grumbled.

"Yeah, sure." Hailey laughed, thinking I couldn't be serious. Usually, I want to be as close to Michael Lawrence as possible. Then she looked at me and saw I wasn't joking. "Whoa, what's up?" she asked.

"Let's just get a spot and I'll tell you everything."

In silence we walked to a table at the opposite side of the cafeteria from Michael. We wedged ourselves at the very end of the table, leaving a gap between us and a group of eighth graders sitting at the other end. As soon as we were seated, I began venting, filling Hailey in on the whole annoying story.

"That is a bummer," she agreed when I'd finished.

I paused to slurp my soup, and she took a mouthful of rice, chewing thoughtfully. Then she said, "I guess you can see this as an opportunity, though, if you look at it one way."

"How? It's nothing but the end, as far as I can see," I said miserably.

"Well, now you get to find out for sure if Michael likes you or not. It also gives him a chance to see what it's like without you around and available all the time. You get to play hard to get without even trying!"

"Well, it's not like I have all that much else going on. I mean, besides my article and—" I gulped. I'd almost said, *Dear Know-It-All.*

"And what?" asked Hailey suspiciously.

"And . . ." Mentally, I skimmed the calendar of upcoming school events that we'd reviewed for coverage in our staff meeting. "And gymnastics team tryouts!" I blurted. Uh-oh. I regretted it as soon as I'd said it. ***Journalist Can't Keep Quiet, Trouble Ensues!***

"Gymnastics team!" Hailey looked confused for a moment, then her face cleared and she smiled a megawatt grin. "Yay, Sammy! You go, girl!"

Let me just say right now, as an aside, that Hailey is a superjock and I am a super-not. She is cocaptain of the girls' varsity soccer team, even though she's only in seventh grade, and she plays all year round (something called Futsal in the winter). She has two older brothers, and all they do in her family is play sports outdoors and then go home and play sports indoors on the Xbox and Wii. She is always trying to get me to try out for the soccer team, but as I point out, I would not make *her* team, so what would be the point? Anything with footwork is my main problem. I am a klutz who trips over everything (Michael even changed my nickname from "Pasty" to "Trippy" a while back after a couple of particularly clumsy days).

But I do have a little secret, and Hailey knows it: I am really good on the uneven parallel bars.

I know, right? Go figure. It's such a random

skill, and certainly not that useful. Kind of like a party trick. Most people have no idea I can do it. Sometimes even I forget, but then we have the gymnastics unit for the trimester and I ace the bars, people are wowed for a few days, and then everyone forgets again.

Actually, I guess it's not totally random because my perfect older sister, Allie, was the star of the Cherry Valley Middle School gymnastics team a few years back. In fact, each time the gymnastics coaches hear my name, their faces light up, hoping I'm made of the same star material as my sister. But then I try a floor routine or the balance beam (both of which require, um, walking), and I trip and mess up and generally make a fool out of myself, and everyone realizes again that I'm not Allie.

The truth is, I have always harbored a secret desire to try out, and Hailey is aware of this. But now I wish I hadn't opened my mouth because I know she will go on another crusade to get me to try out, just like she did last year.

"Ohhhh, this is good. This is gonna be great!" Hailey rubbed her hands together and wiggled excitedly in her seat. "I can train you! I can get you ready. When do tryouts start?" she asked eagerly. "How much time do I have?"

"They start next Friday," I said without enthusiasm. "So you'd better get cracking."

"Great. That gives us some time. We can do this! You can make it! It's all in the mind-set, you know. You have to think like a winner. Okay, here's what I do. . . ."

Now, there is nothing more boring to me than hearing about practicing for sports. It's like hearing people talk about their dreams from the night before. Yawn! I knew Hailey was only being a good friend, but my attention started to wander. And it wandered right over to Michael Lawrence, who caught my eye and then had the nerve to smile and wave at me!

Why did I have to look at him in the first place!

"Ugh!" I said out loud, interrupting Hailey's monologue.

"What?" she said.

"Oh, sorry. I just . . . Michael caught me looking at him. Then he smiled and waved."

"So wave back, you idiot!" said Hailey.

"Why? I'm mad at him!"

"Just wave. You still love him! You can deal with the mad part another time. Come on! Wave or I'll do it for you!"

Visions of Hailey grabbing my hand and conducting a false wave made me shudder. I figured I'd better do it myself.

I looked at Michael again and tried to catch his eye. When he glanced my way, I did a quick nerdy wave, and I think he saw me but I wasn't sure. Anyway, that was good enough.

"Satisfied?" I said to Hailey.

"Not really," she said. "I hope you try harder than that for your spot on the gymnastics team."

I felt deflated. I knew she was right. Why did I always make such a mess out of everything?

Hailey turned and looked over her shoulder at Michael's table.

"Stop!" I hissed. "Don't look! He'll think I care!"

"You *do* care!" Hailey hissed back. "Anyway, he's standing up and . . . he's looking at you and . . . he's walking right this way!"

"What do I say?!"

"Just . . . act natural."

My heart was racing.

"Pasty?"

It was him!

Chapter 2

JOURNALIST THROWS UP AT LUNCH, BECOMES SOCIAL OUTCAST

★ ★ ★

Casually, I looked up, reining in my nerves and trying to play it cool.

"Oh, hey, Michael."

"What, I'm not Mikey anymore?" he teased, his blue eyes crinkling at the corners in a smile.

"Mikey" is his family nickname (I heard his mom use it once), and I usually call him that when he calls me "Pasty" or whatever annoying nickname he's given me that day.

"Oh, yeah. Sorry, Mikey," I said. Hailey glared at me. Even I knew I was being grumpy, but I couldn't help it.

"So what are you two plotting?" Michael asked, turning to include Hailey in his smile.

"Sammy's gymnastics team tryouts!" she said with a huge grin.

"Hailey!" I cried, horrified. **Reporter Fires Best Friend,** I thought.

"That's great, Sam!" said Michael, turning back to me again. "I didn't know you were into gymnastics."

There are a lot of things you don't know about me, I wanted to say. But instead, I said something brilliant like, "Well, yeah. Um."

"She's just being modest," bragged Hailey on my behalf. "You should see her on the uneven bars! She's incredible!"

"Really?" said Michael. Did I mention he's a major jock too? I'm forever waiting for him to finish one practice or another so we can work on an article. (He's a second-string quarterback on the varsity football team, the star pitcher of the varsity baseball team, and he plays varsity basketball as a hobby.)

Suddenly, I came to, remembering why we were even talking about the gymnastics team tryouts. "Well, I wouldn't say incredible, but all I know is, I'm going to be very, very busy these next few weeks, with training and tryouts and whatever. . . ."

"Great!" said Michael.

Wait, *great*? That wasn't good.

"Let me know if you want any help training," he added.

I felt a little better, but then Hailey jumped in. "Oh no. I'm her trainer. I'll be running this show. You just stay out of it, Lawrence." Those two are always trying to out-jock each other, comparing skills and calling each other by last names and stuff.

I stared daggers at Hailey, trying to get her to back down. Didn't she realize Michael was offering an opening? Usually, she was the one reading his signals right, but this time she missed it. This was so annoying!

"Well, if I have some time, I might contact you for some of your fancy . . . warm-up ideas or something," I said. "But otherwise, I will be very, very busy."

"Okay, well . . . good luck, then. I guess I'll see you around." And he walked off.

As soon as he was out of earshot, Hailey and I both began yelling at each other at the same time.

"Couldn't you tell he was disappointed you didn't call him by his little nickname? And then he offered to train you!" ranted Hailey.

"Which you turned down on my behalf—thanks a lot!" I fumed.

And back and forth we went until we were spent. Then we both just sat there playing with our food. It was time to go, but we weren't moving.

Suddenly, someone came up behind us and said, "Hey, baby. Where have *you* been all day?"

Baby?

I turned around to see Danny Burke, an eighth grader who'd just transferred into Cherry Valley Middle School this fall. But who was he talking to?

I turned to ask Hailey, and there she was, looking up at him all starry-eyed with her mouth hanging open. *What?*

"Hey . . . Danny," she replied. She reached up and fluffed her blond hair, which she always does when she's nervous or flirting. *Wait a minute . . .*

"What are you two girls up to?" he asked,

coming around the table so we could both look at him head-on.

"Oh, the usual," said Hailey, batting her eyes.

Danny Burke has a very cute face: big brown eyes, a button nose, lots of freckles, bright white teeth, and medium brown hair that sticks up in kind of a grown-out crew cut with a big cowlick in the front. Basically, he looks like an overgrown adorable six-year-old. But he obviously has a ton of confidence. Danny looked at me and gave me a big wink. It was pretty funny, actually. I looked to Hailey to share a little private smile with her, but she couldn't stop staring at him.

OMG, she likes him! I realized. *Okay, Martone,* I told myself. *Play it cool.* I knew to tread carefully. Hailey's crushes were not easy things to navigate.

"So . . . what's going on? Got any weekend plans?" he asked Hailey, cracking his knuckles.

I winced. I couldn't help it. Knuckle cracking skeeves me out.

"Maybe . . . maybe not. You?" said Hailey. (I wanted to shake the body snatcher who had taken over Hailey and yell, *Who are you, and what have you done with my best friend?*)

Danny reached over and grabbed a saltine from Hailey's tray. "Not sure. Let's do something. I'll IM you later," he said, munching the cracker for emphasis. "K?"

Hailey nodded. "I'm up for anything," she said.

Danny grinned, gave me another big cheesy wink, then turned and strolled away.

Journalist Throws Up at Lunch, Becomes Social Outcast.

Hailey just sat there, smiling.

"Hailey, hello? Are you out of your mind?" I said.

"Oh, I just think he's so cute! Don't you?" she said, all dreamy.

Oh boy. I looked up at the big clock on the cafeteria wall. We were going to be late for our next class: earthonomics for me and language arts for Hailey. "Hailey, we have to go. We've got some major stuff to discuss later, though. What are you up to?"

"Meet me after futsal practice," she said.

That would be in the gym, since it's *indoor*

soccer season now. "Fine. See you then," I said. At least it would give me a chance to stop by the newspaper office when it was quiet so I could grab my Know-It-All letters out of my mailbox.

Hailey has had some pretty lame boy situations this year. I thought about them as I walked to class. First she had a crush on *my* crush, Michael Lawrence. *Hel-lo?* Not gonna happen! Then she decided she liked this other boy, Scott Parker. But he had a stalker (yes, a stalker!), and so he wasn't really interested in going out with anyone. At the last school dance, she danced with Frank Duane, who totally liked her, but she didn't like him. Sometimes I think Hailey only wants what she can't have. And now she likes this . . . Romeo.

I was so distracted thinking of Hailey's love life that I tripped over a garbage can (how did I miss a garbage can?), and two eighth-grade guys walking behind me laughed and whistled. Argh! I had to bow so they wouldn't think I was hurt or a loser. It's hard work being klutzy, but I'm pretty good at it by now.

★ ★ ★

That afternoon I stopped by the newspaper office on my way to Hailey's boring practice. Inside, no one was there, not even Mr. Trigg. That was probably a good thing, because I am still so annoyed at him for separating my dream team for the next issue that I might not have been so friendly.

I swiftly locked the door to the hall, then swooped over to the Dear Know-It-All mailbox and grabbed the four letters inside, shoving them deep into my messenger bag. Then I unlocked the door and exited, cool as a cucumber. I'm getting better and better at all this sneaky stuff, which I'm not sure is a good thing!

In the gym, I sat in the bleachers and did some homework, reading about natural disasters, freak weather, and shark attacks and their effects on tourism for my earthonomics class. It was actually pretty interesting stuff. When I'd gotten as far as I could in my homework without a computer, I still had half an hour to kill before Hailey would be done, so I decided to take a peek into the gymnastics room next door.

Looking around, the first thing I noticed was a

large poster on the wall. It read:

GYMNASTICS TEAM TRYOUTS IN TWO WEEKS!

Levels 1 through 4
Small gymnasium
Open practice sessions weekdays
after school and Saturdays
All are welcome

And then it gave the tryout details for each team level and what was required.

I could probably make the Level One team, I thought, surveying the mild requirements of cartwheeling on the floor mat and a straight jump on the vault. You only needed to participate in three of the five events (floor, vault, bars, trampoline, and beam). But the Level One gymnasts would all be sixth graders for sure, and it would stink to be stuck with them. I'd have to try for Level Two, and that would be quite a bit harder.

I bit my lip, studying the list for a minute. Then I sighed and decide to give things a whirl. I looked around. There were two coaches busy with a couple of other girls at the opposite end of the gym. Coach Lunetta, who was Allie's coach, glanced my way and waved and then went back to work. I was relieved. I didn't want anybody observing me—not yet. I just needed to know if this was even worth a try. "Girls, make sure you have a spotter before you start working out!" Coach called.

After I did my usual stretching exercises to warm up, I crossed over the springy floor exercise mat and passed the big clunky vault, the high and low balance beams, and then the trampoline set into the floor. I had eyes only for my favorite piece of equipment: the uneven parallel bars. There was a girl sitting next to them. "Want me to spot you?" she asked.

I paused. "Sure," I said. I mean, I was already there.

I adjusted the bar heights, gave the mat underneath a quick lift and drop to fluff it, then I chalked my hands from the chalk bin on the floor and stepped into position underneath the top bar. Grasping the wood with both hands evenly spaced, I swung myself once, twice, then three times, keeping my body taut but flexible, just like I had learned. Then I snapped my feet onto the lower bar, flipped over so I was facedown, and did a quick flip over the top bar, just to warm up. I flipped one more time over the top bar, landed my feet on the lower bar, then slid down and hooked my legs over the lower bar, swinging off into a perfect penny drop. I stuck the landing, my feet a little unsteady on the squishy mat, then I did a pretend bow for the pretend adoring Olympic judges.

"Nice job!" said my spotter, stepping back.

I was breathing hard, but it had felt so good to do something physical so well. It made me excited and left me wanting more. A good time to stop, in my book.

"Thanks," I said. I crossed the room to the low beam and did a few laps back and forth across it, dipping my toes, trying a small hop, but terrified to do much else. Some girls can execute a back walkover, or even a flip called a salto, on the beam with ease. To me, that would mean sudden, certain death, or at least maiming—if not of myself, then of a spectator. I bounced over to the runway for the vault. Coach Lunetta was standing there to spot. She nodded at me. "Nice to see you!" she said. I guess she remembered me from Allie's meets.

I drew my heels tightly together, stood tall, and raised my hand in an imaginary ready salute for the nonexistent judges. Coach smiled at me. "You're good to go!" Then I sprinted down the run-up area, bounced onto the springboard, and—*Oof!*

My body landed smack against the horse, taking the wind out of me. I'd forgotten to check the springboard's distance from the horse, and it was, I guess, a little too far away for me. A rookie mistake, but a klutzy one nonetheless. I felt dispirited and sat for a few minutes, gathering my strength and my dignity from the floor. Klutzy, klutzy.

"Are you okay?" asked Coach Lunetta.

"Oh, yeah," I said, dusting myself off. "I'm totally fine. I do that all the time." Which I realized was kind of a stupid thing to say to a coach who may or may not be choosing you for a team.

I wasn't so sure I'd be trying out for the gymnastics team after all.

It was time to go. I hoisted my bruised body

and ego up and lumbered back to the door where I'd entered. I jammed my feet back into my clogs, picked up my bag and my coat, and tucked my shirt back in. After one last backward glance, I went to pick up the real athlete from her practice.

Rookie Takes Early Retirement, Leaves Competition to the Pros.

Chapter 3

ADVICE COLUMNIST SHOWS EXTREME LACK OF SENSITIVITY

★ ★ ★

"Come on!" Hailey was dragging me with all of her might. She was on a post-exercise high, having raced around the gym for the past hour. It was a very common thing for Hailey. She's always all happy and wild after sports. And now she wanted me to go back to the gymnastics room and practice.

But I was on a postexercise low, which was common for me. All I wanted to do was go home and read a few news blogs. "How are you ever going to get better if you don't practice?" she insisted.

"I did practice! I'm still great on the bars."

"Look, what do you need to be able to do for the tryouts?" she asked, standing with her hands on her hips in a challenging posture.

"Well . . ." I sighed. I didn't really want to get back into it and encourage her to start up some big training session.

Hailey tapped her foot on the floor. "I'm waiting..."

"Fine," I snapped. I led her back to the door to the small gymnasium and gestured at the flyer. "It's all there," I said. There was still a group of girls in there practicing on the equipment.

Hailey read the gymnastics poster slowly and carefully. Whether it was because she has dyslexia, or because she wanted to make sure she got it all, or because she was trying to torture me—or maybe all three—it dragged on.

"Hailey!" I said impatiently.

"Which level are you going for?" she asked, not turning from the poster.

"Two, I guess," I mumbled, dreading her ever-competitive response.

"Two!" Hailey exploded, turning around. "Two?"

Her reaction annoyed me. I nodded defiantly. "Yes. Two."

"Why not four?"

I knew it would come to that. "Because in case

you hadn't noticed, I am not a gymnast. Level Four is for girls who have been doing this for years! I'd kill myself if I tried any of that. Literally, dead."

Hailey sighed and returned to the flyer once more. "I can see we have our work cut out for us," she said finally. "Level Two it is."

"You know, I'm not even sure I can do any of that stuff," I admitted. "Maybe I should try for—"

"Shh! Stop right there. You aren't joining a team of all sixth graders, that's for sure. I wouldn't let you, even if you made it."

I smiled. "Okay."

"So show me what you can do from this list."

"What?" I said, panicking.

"I've got all night," said Hailey, grabbing a seat on a folding chair against the wall. "Go for it. Show me everything you've got."

"Well, that shouldn't take long," I said. I kicked off my clogs and began my circuit, making sure to move the springboard closer to the vault this time. At this point, there was a spotter at each station. They looked like older high school girls who were helping out the middle school team. *Great,* I thought.

All I need is word of this getting back to Allie.

I did one or two very basic tricks on each apparatus: a front flip on the trampoline, a sequence of cartwheels on the floor, a back hip circle with a push-away dismount on bars, a straight jump with a pivot turn for the vault. Hailey had lots of comments on my form and my bravery. She kept hopping up to consult the flyer on the wall and see how advanced I was, compared to the outlined levels and their required tricks. It was kind of annoying that she'd suddenly become a professional gymnastics coach, but she did have a pretty good eye for form. I'd listen and nod and try again, just once, then I'd move on. We didn't have all night, no matter what Hailey said.

And then it was time to try the beam. I'd saved the worst for last.

I was trying to calm my nerves and not look down. *Journalist Dies in Tragic Beam Fall* would be a very sad headline. Cautiously, I tried a couple of cute jumps, barely landing the second one. I teetered for a moment to catch my balance.

"You can do it, Sammy!" hollered Hailey.

I took a deep breath. A cartwheel was the natural next step. I'd already done a bunch on the floor, so how hard could it be? I put down one hand, then the other, kicked up my legs and . . . I was over! I did it! I teetered again on the landing and, at the last second, let myself fall off. It was a controlled fall, though, onto a mat, so I didn't get hurt—not physically, at least. But my ego sure was hurt when the next thing I heard was a loud whistle and then some clapping.

"Way to go, Pasty!"

My stomach dropped. I jumped up from where I'd been sitting on the mat, replaying my performance in my mind. Michael Lawrence was standing in his basketball uniform at the door to the gymnastics room. I felt myself go beet red, and I wanted to die right then and there. Why, oh why, couldn't he have seen me on the uneven bars? Why did he have to see me on my worst apparatus?

"Shut up, Lawrence," said Hailey. "I'd like to see you try a cartwheel on a beam three feet in the air!"

"Don't worry, I wouldn't! I wasn't making fun

of Pasty. I'm just impressed she'd even try such a crazy thing."

Crossing the room toward him, I couldn't tell if he was teasing me. As I drew closer, his smile confused me. I tilted my head and looked at him.

He put his palms up in a pose of mock surrender. "Honest!" he said.

Hailey and I looked at each other, as if weighing his words.

"You should see her on the uneven bars," said Hailey.

"I'd love to!" said Michael. My heart leapt. "But I have practice now and I'm already late, so I can't stay. I'm sorry. Can I come back another day? Will you be here?"

"No," I said. "Don't come back. I need to practice in private," I said.

I could feel Hailey staring daggers at me, but I wasn't trying to be mean. I knew what I was doing. The last thing I needed while I was practicing was to worry about Michael Lawrence spontaneously appearing to watch me! Then I'd never try anything, for fear of potentially making a fool of myself.

"Oh, okay," he said, backing away.

I felt bad. It had come out wrong, and now it looked like I'd hurt his feelings. I didn't know what to say. *Advice Columnist Shows Extreme Lack of Sensitivity.*

Hailey butted in. "What my friend Miss Rude means is that when she is ready, she will let you know, and then you can come see. Right, Sam?"

I nodded. "Right. Come back. For sure," I said weakly.

Michael nodded, waved, and took off.

"Nice," said Hailey, watching him go. "Really nice."

"Oh, whatever," I said angrily. I didn't need Hailey critiquing my crush behavior right now. "You're my gymnastics trainer, not my love life trainer," I said.

Hailey looked at me in surprise. "So I'm hired?"

I nodded, studying the flyer again. "Yeah. We'll train, but there's no guarantee I'll actually try out, okay?"

"Oh, you'll try out, all right. Just you wait and see," said Hailey.

Suddenly, Coach Lunetta was at the door. "Girls, I have to close up the gym for the night, so you'll have to leave now. I can't let you use the equipment without supervision. But leading up to tryouts, we'll have a coach here every afternoon and all day Saturday."

"Okay, Coach," I said.

"You Martones are all alike! Can't keep you out of here!" she teased with a smile. "Now go!" And she fake swatted us out the door and turned out the lights.

We left, giggling, but I felt a nervous flutter in my stomach at being compared to Allie yet again.

That night after dinner, I went up to my desk to organize my homework and do one last check of my favorite news websites. One of my teachers at journalism camp last summer told me that if you want to be an informed and impartial reporter, you need to "consume" news media from a minimum of three different sources a day. That way, you'll get a more balanced view of the issues and you'll get closer to the truth, because every article contains the writer's slant or opinion in one way or another, whether the writer meant to include it or not. It's just in what you choose to add and what you choose to leave out that the information in the article becomes tailored a certain way. I loved learning that.

Anyway, after checking out the websites for the *Huffington Post*, *CNN*, *Fox News*, the *Daily Beast*, *People* magazine, my local newspaper, Allie's school (she runs the website), and a few others, I was ready to close up shop for the night. It was time to take a peek at the Dear Know-It-All letters. I shut down my computer (that draining whir of the fan shutting off is the saddest sound of my day) and opened the first letter. It was written on graph paper, and it said:

Dear Know-It-All,

I have a lot of collections, but my mom says my room is a mess and wants me to get rid of everything. I've spent a lot of time gathering these things, and I like them. What should I do?

From,

Messy But Happy

Hmm. That was a pretty good one. I set it aside and opened the next one, which was written on pink Hello Kitty stationery:

Dear Know-It-All,

Am I weird? I still love my Barbies. I don't act out dumb pretend stories with them, but I do like to dress them up and set up their Dream House and stuff. My friends don't know I still do this. I know I'm too old, but it's fun. My older brother teases me and says it's time to throw them away. What do you think?

Signed,

Barbie Girl

Oh, I could relate to that. Allie and I loved our Barbies for a long time, but somewhere along the way, we stopped playing with them. I don't know why. Maybe Allie did and I just followed suit, like usual. I think my mom still has them in the attic. Not that I'd take them out. I mean, if they were still lying around, it might be fun to put an outfit together. Like maybe that cute denim dress she had. . . . Yeah, this could be another good letter. I set it aside.

The next one was boring. It was about how to get more sleep. But the fourth and final one really caught my attention. Written on simple blue stationery in a matching envelope, it read:

Dear Know-It-All,

I'm in seventh grade, and I really, really want to try out for the gymnastics team, but I don't know if I have what it takes. I've taken some classes at the Y, so I'm okay at some of the things like the beam, but I stink at the bars. I'm too embarrassed to try out at school where people I know can see me. I'd be so humiliated if I fell or got hurt during tryouts. I'm already really shy as it is. What should I do?

Signed,

Gymnastics Team Hopeful

I sat back in my desk chair and swiveled a little from side to side as I thought. It was like this girl was a mind reader, except her issue was with bars not beam. I was dying to know who'd written it. Maybe we should team up and train together. I drummed my fingers on my desk as I tried to think of who it could be.

"Girls! Bedtime!" my mom called up the stairs. Sighing, I folded the letters up and put them back in their envelopes, then back in my big Dear Know-It-All folder. Then I leaned over to wedge it behind my desk so my snooping sister wouldn't find it.

Naturally, it was just as I was tucking the packet behind the desk that Allie walked in, knocking as she opened the door.

"Allie, knocking isn't really polite if you do it *while* you're opening the door," I said with exasperation. Now I'd have to find *another* new hiding place.

Allie looked at me suspiciously. "What are you hiding back there?"

Reminding myself that it's easier to hide things in plain sight, I held up the folder. "I'm not hiding anything. My newspaper clippings file slid down behind the desk. I was *retrieving* it," I told her.

"Oh, can I see your articles?"

This girl *has* to work for the CIA when she grows up.

"No," I said. "What's up?"

"I heard on Buddybook that you're trying out for the gym team," she said.

"What?! That's insane! How would that get out?" I cried.

"So it's true?" she said.

"Yes, but . . ."

Allie turned to leave, conversation over. "Thank you!" she singsonged. "Next time, might be nice to tell your own family first, before everyone else." Then she closed the door.

I shook my head. I couldn't believe this was happening. Reason number 512 that I hate Buddybook. It knows you're going to do things before *you* even do, and then it tells everyone! *Journalist Sues Buddybook, Loses.*

I hid the Dear Know-It-All folder underneath my socks in my top drawer, then I went to the bathroom to get ready for bed. A few minutes later, I was in my pj's, doing my assigned "independent" reading, when my mom came in to say good night.

"So Allie told me you're trying out for the gymnastics team, honey! That's great news!"

"Aargh!" I threw my book across the room.

"What?" said my mom, innocently (for real).

"Oh, never mind. Yes. I am. Or, I'm thinking about it anyway."

"That's wonderful. You can do anything you put your mind to, Sam Martone. You know that, right, sweetheart?"

"Thanks, Mom." We hugged and she turned out the light. I snuggled down and wound up dreaming that I was competing against Barbie for a spot on the gymnastics team in a room filled with someone's Hello Kitty collection. Weird.

Chapter 4

DREAMS OF OLYMPIC HOPEFUL DASHED BY MIDDLE SCHOOL SQUAD

★ ★ ★

The next day I began interviewing eighth graders for my article on their memories of Cherry Valley Middle School. I was glad to have something to do so I wouldn't be focusing on Michael Lawrence strategizing with Austin Carey in the cafeteria. I was also glad that I got to choose the order in which I interviewed the subjects, because there was at least one of them I was dreading.

When Susannah had made the list of eighth-grade interviewees and e-mailed it to me, it looked like a pretty well-rounded lineup at first glance. But then one name jumped out at me: Danny Burke! I immediately replied to Susannah that I didn't think he was a good choice, but she got right back to me saying he was the only new eighth grader this year and she really wanted that perspective. She added that he was pretty cute so maybe I wouldn't mind, and then she put a little smiley icon at the end of her e-mail. I wanted to puke, but I knew then that I was stuck, since the editor in chief is the boss.

Cintra Noble was a "cool" eighth grader, and I was a little nervous about approaching her. But she'd been friendly in our e-mail exchange and had readily agreed to meet me. I knew some people loved being interviewed and others hated it. I hoped Cintra would be somewhere in the middle.

At lunchtime, we grabbed sandwiches and met on a bench in the hall outside the library. I ate my sandwich one-handed while I took notes in my trusty spiral-bound reporter's notebook. I had prepared a list of questions for my interview subjects, including *Who was the strictest teacher you had at Cherry Valley? Which class do you think will be the most useful in your life? What was your favorite lunch menu item in the cafeteria?* Stuff like that.

At first, Cintra was a little quiet—giving short

answers, not really elaborating on anything. But I encouraged her, and after a while, she relaxed and began to talk more. I wondered what she'd be like if her friends were there, or a boy. Lots of times, that makes people act differently.

It turned out Cintra had moved here in sixth grade, so she hadn't known anyone when she started at Cherry Valley Middle. As we talked, she told me more about how shy she'd felt in the beginning and how she had only hung out with the one or two people who'd been nice to her but didn't share any of her interests. She'd been really sad.

"I wish I hadn't been so nervous when I was the new kid. I wasted so much time feeling sorry for myself back then when I could have been making new friends."

I nodded, copying down what would prove to be a great quote. I looked up to see a new girl from *my* grade, Jenna Palmer, walking by. I smiled and waved, and Cintra looked up and smiled too.

Jenna looked panicked, like she couldn't quite believe I was waving at *her.* I watched her struggle with whether or not she should look over her shoulder to see if I was waving at someone else, and she finally gave up and made a tiny wave back. I felt bad. How was it that more than four months of the school year had gone by and I had never really talked to this girl?

After she'd entered the library, I pointed my thumb at the door and whispered to Cintra, "Also a new girl."

Cintra nodded. "I could tell. That's how I was. Scared of my own shadow. Dying for friends and wishing I knew how to make some."

I made a mental note to make a bigger effort the next time I saw Jenna.

"Any other thoughts on your time here?" I asked, beginning to wrap things up with Cintra.

"It has been great. I hope the kids here know what a great school they've got and that they take advantage of everything the place has to offer. If you feel intimidated here, you shouldn't. Just imagine what things will be like when you get to a huge high school or college! Better to gain your confidence now." She smiled, and I stuck out my hand to shake hers.

"Great interview. You're going to be hard to top!" I said.

"Thanks," said Cintra. "I'm sure you've got some other interesting people coming up."

I scanned the list. "A good mix," I said. "It should be a pretty good article."

"I can't wait to read it."

We said good-bye, and I dumped the remains of my lunch before going to the library for the remaining fifteen minutes of my free time.

Inside, I crossed to the wall of computers. There was only one available, and Jenna was sitting at the console right next to it, looking at something on Wikipedia.

"Hey," I said, sitting down.

She smiled nervously at me. "Hi," she said, and looked back at her computer screen.

"What are you working on?" I asked, thinking of how Cintra had felt when she was new—eager for friends but unsure of how to break in.

"Oh, it's for a paper for earthonomics," she said.

"Cool. I love that class," I said. "I'm Sam, by the way. Sam Martone."

"I know. I'm Jenna Palmer," she said.

"Nice to meet you, officially."

I turned to my computer and logged on. I wanted to go to the USA Gymnastics website and see if I could watch some videos of routines. Hailey was meeting me in the gymnastics room after school to help me practice, and she said my assignment was to come armed with a list of moves I wanted to learn. How a soccer player was going to coach me, I had no idea, but just the very knowledge that someone would be waiting for me so I couldn't bag my practice made a lot of sense. Otherwise, I just wouldn't go.

I logged on, and one link led to another, until pretty soon I was watching Olympic routines on YouTube. Jenna stood up to leave, and I paused the video to say good-bye.

"Oh, cool! I'm obsessed with gymnastics!" she said, looking over my shoulder. "Can you push play, just for a minute?"

Smiling, I agreed, and we watched in silence as Gabby Douglas executed a perfect backflip on the balance beam.

"Wow," sighed Jenna when it was over. "I so wish I had the nerve to do that. I've taken classes, but I pretty much stink."

"I know. Me too," I said.

"If we could do *that*, we'd be the stars of the gymnastics team!" Jenna giggled. Suddenly, something clicked in my mind. Jenna: petite, fit, interested in gymnastics, shy, the word "stink" to describe her abilities. It had to be! I almost came right out and asked her if she'd written a letter to the school paper, but then I would have revealed that I was Dear Know-It-All. There must be a subtle way to find out.

"Hey, are you . . . ," I began. But then I was rudely interrupted.

"What's up, girls?" It was Danny Burke.

"Hi," I said, immediately annoyed.

But Jenna blushed. "Hey, Danny," she said.

He pointed at her and gave her a thumbs-up. "Lookin' good today. So what's going on? Any weekend plans?"

Jenna blushed even harder and looked down at her shoes. "Oh, I don't know. Maybe."

What was it with this guy? Why did he make perfectly normal girls lose their brains when he was around? And why didn't I feel the same way? ***Journalist's Resistance to Romeo's Charms Puzzles Locals.***

"I'll IM you," he said. And then he winked at both of us, and walked away.

I didn't know Jenna well enough to say anything bad about Danny, but I was dying to ask her what she saw in that guy. He was such a phony! He'd said the exact same thing to Hailey! But Jenna stood there watching him walk away, a big smile on her face.

"Wow," I said tentatively. But Jenna didn't catch my sarcasm.

"I know," she said, as if agreeing with my amazement at his awesomeness.

O-kayy . . .

The bell rang and lots of people stood up. I had to get going because my next class was clear on the other side of the building. I'd missed my chance to find out more about Jenna and whether she'd written the Dear Know-It-All letter.

"Well, see ya," I said.

"Yeah. Thanks for sharing the video. I love watching anything that has to do with gymnastics. It definitely inspired me."

Inspired her! Ha! So there! It *was* her. It had to be.

Wow, I am getting really good at this Dear Know-It-All thing, I thought, walking away. I decided that hers was the letter I'd run for the next issue. And I'd write a great response. It was the least I could do to make a new girl feel more at home.

"Bye!" I called, and I sprinted off to my class.

Later that day Hailey and I were walking to her practice, where I would do my homework until she was free to train me at four. She was in her usual jock clothes (sweats, long-sleeved T-shirt), while I was in a skirt and sweater with my gymnastics outfit balled up in my messenger bag.

"Okay, so I did a lot of research online, and I spent some time on Buddybook asking around about gymnastics routines and levels and school tryouts . . ." Hailey was being all official, and it was kind of irritating. After all, I'd made her my trainer, but it wasn't like I'd made her my boss! "And here's the plan. An hour and a half of practice a day, every day, for the next nine days. Plus, homework: studying videos online, reading the gymnastics tips on these websites"—she handed me a printed list—"and this workout regimen at home." She handed me another printout.

"Phew, that's a lot," I said skeptically.

"That's not all," said Hailey. "Here's your diet plan. You need to bulk up those muscles a little, so I want you drinking protein shakes. And make sure you pick up some flaxseed and omega-3 oils at the health-food store, and add some form of lean protein to every meal. Here are some suggestions." She handed me yet another printed sheet.

"Hailey! Whoa! Slow down! What's up with all this? I'm not even totally sure I'm going to try out!"

Hailey kind of came to, like she'd been in a coaching daze. "What? Yes you are."

"But I don't know if I'm good enough!" I protested.

"Well, if you follow these plans, you will be," she said.

"Hailey, listen. I am not an athlete. I think we both know that by now. If, by some miracle, I can pull together a routine that is snappy and clean enough for me to try out with, I will do it. But even if I make the team, I might not join. I've been pretty clear about that from the get-go. I'll never be as good as the other girls, and it might be very stressful. Got it?"

Hailey waved her hand breezily. "Details," she said. "Once I've trained you, you'll be ready. You'll make it, you'll join it, and you'll love it. I promise, or I'm not the best darned coach you'll ever have!"

I bit my lip. If I didn't make it, I didn't know who'd be more disappointed: me or Hailey. **_Dreams of Olympic Hopeful Dashed by Middle School Squad_**, I thought. And I didn't mean the athlete. I meant the coach.

"Well, all I'm saying is, we'll see," I said.

"You sound like my mom," grumbled Hailey, heading off to dump her book bag in the locker room.

★ ★ ★

Later, as we struggled over my vault sequence, I heard the gym door open. *Oh no!* I thought. *Please don't let it be Michael!*

But it was Kristen Durkin, a nice girl from my class that I'd never really gotten to know. We waved across the gym, and she started stretching. She's on the gymnastics team already, I think, so she was probably just getting back into the swing of things.

"Focus," said Hailey.

"I am!" I protested.

Hailey consulted a gymnastics book she had checked out of the library. "Okay, the vault run is about getting enough speed to hit the springboard with the force you need to propel you over the table and through your trick."

I rolled my eyes. "I know. Run fast, hit hard, go high," I said.

"Right!" Hailey smiled as if proud of herself for how quickly I was catching on.

"That's, like, lesson number one in beginner gymnastics," I said. She was being such a know-it-all (ha-ha) that I wouldn't give her the satisfaction of thinking she'd taught me something I already knew.

I glanced over at Kristen, who had checked in with Coach Lunetta and was now on the high balance beam. She steadied herself and then did a handstand into a roundoff dismount, perfectly sticking the finish.

"Wow," I breathed.

"How come you can't do that?" whispered Hailey at my side.

I elbowed her. "'Cause I have a lousy coach!"

"Very funny," she said. "Not. Now come on."

I have to admit that the day's practice was productive, and it was inspiring to watch a real member of the team doing such neat tricks. I didn't get a chance to see Kristen on the bars, which I would have loved, but I was already trying to come up with a plan for how I could get her to train me on the beam without hurting Hailey's feelings.

We wrapped up early because I had a test the next day, but Kristen stayed on, practicing. Leaving, we walked past the boys' basketball team practice, and I slowed my pace to see if I could spot Michael.

"There he is!" I whispered to Hailey.

He was off to the side breathing hard, all sweaty and cute, his hands on his knees as he tried to catch his breath. I waved but he didn't see me. I considered staying to watch, but there's kind of an unwritten rule at our school that anyone can go to games for opposite-sex teams, but you can only watch practices if you're actually dating someone on the team. I didn't want anyone to get the wrong idea, so I took one last long look and I left.

Outside school, Hailey gave me a little pep talk about stretching, conditioning, and eating right. I began to wish I'd started all this jock stuff long ago so that it would be second nature to me by now. It's kind of hard to wedge all this exercise into a life of reading and writing.

Journalist to Jock, in Just One Week!
Nah. Not yet, I decided.

Chapter 5

ADVICE COLUMNIST IN OVER HER HEAD

★ ★ ★

At dinner that night, Allie was full of questions about the gymnastics team. But as it turned out, they were more about her than me.

"So has Coach Adams talked about me a lot?" she asked knowingly.

"Actually . . . ," I said, taking a bite of my broccoli to stretch out the wait. I chewed and swallowed. "I haven't really seen Coach Adams yet, mostly Coach Lunetta. I've just been practicing after school with Hailey."

"Hailey?! What does she know about gymnastics?"

"Nothing, really. She's my trainer, but it's more of an all-around fitness thing. She got a book out of the library for the gymnastics part."

Allie tossed her hair indignantly. "A book?! You can't learn gymnastics from a book!"

"Well . . . I already know a lot of stuff. We're just trying to get ideas for my routines for the tryouts."

"What level are you going for?" asked Allie. "Four?"

I nearly choked on my milk. As I'd already told Hailey, Level Four was more than halfway to the Junior Olympic trials. "No. Um, two. We were thinking Level Two."

"Level Two?" Allie wrinkled her nose in distaste. "I was on Level Two in kindergarten."

I rolled my eyes at my mom. "I know."

"Are you two having fun together, you and Hailey?" my mom asked.

I nodded. "It's okay. Hailey's being a little bossy and kind of a know-it-all."

My mom thought for a second. "You know, it's probably nice for Hailey to have a turn at being the teacher with you as the student for a change, right?" she said.

Hailey always gets extra help from me on her

homework. She also has a tutor. Because of her dyslexia, some subjects are really hard for her, and it takes longer for her to do her schoolwork. I think she feels pretty bad about it. What my mom said actually made a lot of sense.

"You're right," I agreed.

My mom smiled. "So maybe take her being bossy with a grain of salt, if you think she's being a know-it-all." My mom winked at me. Besides Mr. Trigg, she's the only one who knows that I'm Dear Know-It-All this year. I smiled back.

"Are my trophies still there, in the case? The big one from State and the other ones from Regional?" Allie couldn't stop focusing on herself!

"I don't know. I haven't been able to read them because the janitorial staff is obsessed with polishing them," I replied.

Allie looked up quickly, but then realized I was joking. "Whatever. You're just jealous that I had so much success at such a young age."

"Girls," warned my mom. We stopped bickering, but Allie continued to stare menacingly at me. "Allie, it might be nice if you could spend some time with Sam to help her get ready for the tryouts. Maybe meet her at the gymnasium one day and see if you can give her some pointers?"

Allie looked at me. I waited. That could either be very good or very bad. I wasn't sure. "Maybe," she said reluctantly.

I shrugged. *Bad,* I thought. It would be bad. Allie and her entourage at the gym, buttering up the coaches in their office, showing off all her old tricks. Yuck.

"Well, good luck, sweetheart. I know you can do it!" my mom said to me.

"Thanks," I said, staring meaningfully at Allie.

"Whatever," said Allie.

While typing up my notes from my interview with Cintra that night, Hailey IM'd me:

Guess what—danny burke told me I was cute!!!

Wow. Things were really moving along between those two. I wanted to be happy for Hailey, but I really didn't like or trust that guy. I wasn't sure what to say.

Great! When? I typed. Then I chewed my nail while I waited for her reply.

He IM'd me + said what's up 4 the wknd + I said nothing + he said what's a cute girl like u doing w no planz?

I didn't want to encourage her, but she was always so nice about listening to my Michael Lawrence craziness that I knew I had to act kind of excited.

So r u doing something w him?

I tapped my desk, waiting.

I think so.

I had to lie: **Cool!**

And good luck, I added silently.

I sat there thinking afterward. Was I jealous, or did I really not like Danny? *Maybe a little of both.* Did I think he was a bad guy or just wrong for my friend? *Both.* But did I wish Michael would IM me and tell me I was cute? *Yes, definitely!* But it was different with Michael. We had a lot in common. We had a shared history. This Danny Burke was kind of sketchy. I needed to do some research. And as much as I hated to admit it, I needed to do it on Buddybook.

A little while back, I'd gotten in trouble with my mom because I opened a Buddybook account without asking. So I closed it, and then we spent a lot of time talking about Buddybook and online stuff in general. My mom and I made a list of rules that hangs next to my desk, like *Do not post personal information about me or my friends,* and *Do not put up photos without the subjects' permission.* Only when she felt that I really got it all did she let me have a Buddybook account. But the truth is, I really hate Buddybook. I think it's kind of deranged and a time suck, but sometimes . . . well, sometimes it's the only way to find something out. Especially if you're good at snooping.

I logged on and began looking for Danny Burke from Cherry Valley. It didn't take long. His page was public and he had tons of friends. And unsurprisingly, most of them were girls. I scrolled down his wall.

HEY DANNY THANKS 4 THE NOTE! XO LECIA

BIG D! SAVE ME A SEAT ON SATURDAY! ☺ KIMM

PENNY WANTS TO KNOW: WHAT ARE WE DOING FOR YOUR BDAY?!!!

And so on. *Oh, Hailey.* I sighed. She had to have seen this. What was she thinking?

I logged off and shut down my computer, then I spun around in my desk chair and thought and thought. **Advice Columnist in Over Her Head.** Then I spun a little too hard and almost fell over. I was steadying myself on the desk when there was a light tap on the door and my mom came in.

"Hellooo!" she said, smiling.

"Hi," I said.

She sat on the edge of my bed. "Sweetheart, I think Allie is a little hurt that you're taking on this gymnastics tryout without consulting her." She kind of winced as she said it. I guess Allie had given her an earful.

I was annoyed. "It's not like she owns the team," I said.

"No, but come on. That was her whole world for years. She's not being bratty. Honestly, I think she's really hurt. She can't understand why you wouldn't come to her. She wants to be so excited for you, but now she's upset and it's getting in the way."

I was having a hard time picturing Allie wanting

to be excited for me, but whatever. I guess I could understand what my mom was saying.

"So what am I supposed to do?" I asked.

My mom tipped her head to the side. "Don't do it tonight, because then it would be too obvious that we've talked. But in the next day or so, see if you can soften her up by asking a lot of questions. Then wait a little while and invite her to come train you one day next week. I'm sure Hailey would be okay with it. She doesn't mind having Allie around!"

We both laughed at the understatement. Hailey worships the ground Allie walks on.

"Okay," I said. "I just thought she'd make fun of me or something. And I wanted it to be my own thing."

"Sam, honey," my mom said, holding my gaze, "when you made the decision to try out for the team, you have to admit you knew gymnastics was always *Allie's* own thing, right?"

Busted. "Yeah, I guess."

"I'm not saying it's *only* Allie's thing, but she has certainly established herself in that area. Right?"

I nodded, feeling bad. My mom had a point.

"So maybe she feels a little threatened by you too."

That was hard to believe, but I suppose I owed Allie the benefit of the doubt. "Okay. I get it."

She stood up and planted a kiss on the top of my head. "Thanks." She looked at her watch. "Bedtime?"

"Right after I do my squats," I said, hauling myself out of my chair.

The nice part about repetitive exercising—mainly the kind that requires you to count, like squats and sit-ups—is that it makes it hard to think. Or to worry. It definitely had its appeal. The only problem is, it's boring.

Journalist's Brain Turns to Brawn in Quest for Gold.

Oh well, if nothing else, I'd be in pretty good shape by the time these tryouts were over. That is, if I even ended up trying out.

Chapter 6

JOURNALIST WITHHOLDS OPINION: RISKING FRIEND TO SAVE FRIENDSHIP

★ ★ ★

"Hey, Jenna!" I called, spotting Jenna Palmer walking toward me and Hailey in the third-floor hall at school.

She looked up, surprised. "Oh, hey," she said with a shy smile.

We passed and Hailey whispered loudly, "Who was that?"

"Hailey!" I turned around to see if Jenna had heard, but I couldn't tell. "You are the worst whisperer," I said.

Hailey shrugged. "That is *not* something that will keep me up at night. Who is she?"

"Hello?! She's new this year in our grade. Jenna Palmer? Don't you have any classes with her?"

"Nope. She must be smart," Hailey said.

I whacked her arm. "Stop. You're smart. Being dyslexic is just a mechanical problem. Come on."

"Hey, gymnasts," said someone right behind us. Michael!

I spun around, so happy to see him that I had a huge grin plastered on my face.

"Mikey!" I cried, my right sneaker tripping slightly over the back of my left sneaker. I did a little hop to keep my balance.

He looked pleasantly surprised that I was so happy to see him. I had gotten over my anger at not being his writing partner, even though it still smarted a little that he hadn't insisted on it.

"Trippy!" he said, using the nickname he saved for me when I did something klutzy.

"What's up, Lawrence?" asked Hailey.

"Not much. Just basketball and working on the article. It's pretty interesting stuff, actually, Pasty. I wish that—"

"Hey, girl!" interrupted Danny Burke.

Hailey's face turned instantly pink. "Hi!" she said, grinning from ear to ear.

Michael looked perplexed as he watched this exchange.

I wanted the floor to open up and swallow Danny Burke. I was sure Michael had just been about to say he wished I was working on the article with him, and then Danny interrupted. The nerve of this guy!

Danny acknowledged Michael with a nod and me with a wink. Gross. I still hadn't reached out to him about the interview for the article, though all the others were set up. In fact, I had one at lunch today.

"You look slammin' today," said Danny approvingly as he surveyed Hailey from head to toe.

Hailey giggled, speechless.

Now I *knew* this guy was just feeding her lines. Hailey was wearing her usual uniform of sweats (the athletic, useful kind, not the girly, fluffy kind), two T-shirts, a hoodie, and sneakers. She looked cute (Hailey always looks cute!), but "slammin'" seemed a bit over the top.

Michael and I exchanged a look. Then he

shrugged and said, "So how's your article coming along?"

Hailey and Danny began to chat, and I had to stop listening or I would puke.

"Oh, it should be pretty good. I've got an interview today at lunch and a couple of others lined up. And one more I need to book." I rolled my eyes toward Danny to indicate that it was him.

"Seriously?" said Michael. The look of shock on his face was very satisfying.

I nodded.

"Why?" said Michael incredulously.

"Susannah's pick," I said. Then I leaned closer and whispered, "Wants a *new* kid." Mmm. Michael smelled so good up close, like soap and maybe a little bit of Tide detergent. I stepped away, wishing I could go back in for another whiff.

"Wow," said Michael quietly. "Good luck with that."

"Right?" I agreed.

The bell rang and everyone began to move quickly.

"Sorry you can't join me for lunch today," said

Michael. "I'm actually free for once! Bye!" and he dashed off.

Wait! I wanted to yell. *I'll cancel my interview! I'll do whatever it takes! Why didn't you just ask?*

I looked at Hailey and Danny. He touched her arm and said, "I'll catch *you* later!" then he headed to class. As slimy as Danny was, I wished Michael would act that interested in me.

Hailey was in a love fog.

"Earth to Hailey," I said. "We've gotta go. Come home from planet Danny! Hello!"

She snapped out of it enough to trot alongside me to the math department, where our next classes were side by side.

After a few paces, she said, "I can't believe it. Finally! I like a guy and he likes me back! And he's not taken or stalked or weird or anything!" She turned to me with a look of such pure happiness on her face that I knew I could never say anything bad about Danny Burke to her.

Journalist Withholds Opinion: Risking Friend to Save Friendship.

At lunch I spotted Michael sitting with some friends from the basketball team. I wished I could join him and joke around and just be near him. But instead, I had to work.

I scanned the tables for Jimmy Becker, today's interview subject. He was a nice guy, an actor, and I knew him from a couple of school plays I'd seen him in over the past few years. He wasn't "cool" and he wasn't a nerd but right in between. Kind of like me.

I spotted him at a table in the back right corner of the cafeteria and made my way over.

"Hey, Sam!" he said as I arrived.

"Hi, Jimmy. Thanks for meeting me!" His friends scooted over to make more room, and after they all said hi, they pretty much left us alone to talk. I pulled out my notebook and tried to eat my soup left-handed so I could write at the same time.

We chatted aimlessly at first, and then I began working my way down my list of questions: favorite teacher, favorite class, most memorable moment. Jimmy was a great subject. He was funny, opinionated, and not at all shy. I had so many good quotes from him, I wondered if I should pull him out of the article and just write him up as a solo profile.

"Jimmy," I said finally, "I think you're going to be a star. Will you remember me, your first interviewer, when you hit the big time? Will you let me come interview you in your massive hotel suite before the Oscars?"

He laughed. "Anytime. As long as you promise to write only good stuff."

We'd had so much fun that the lunchroom had kind of cleared out around us. I looked at the big clock on the wall. "Oops! Last question! Okay, any parting advice for the younger grades?" I asked.

For once, Jimmy was actually quiet. After a long pause, he said, "I guess . . . I wish I'd gotten started earlier. I wish I had auditioned for the very first play in my first year here, rather than waiting until seventh grade. I really want to be an actor, and it would have been good to get started earlier."

"I don't think the wait held you back at all!" I protested.

"No, but just . . . think of all the fun I missed! All the experience. If I could share a piece of advice, it's to just go for it. If you think something is interesting, give it a try. This is the time and place in your life to do it."

I scrawled the last few words down and snapped my notebook shut. "Great interview!" I said. "Thank you so much!"

"Thank *you!*" said Jimmy. "If you run it, I'll have something for my clipping file."

I stood up with my tray, and something caught my eye across the cafeteria. It was Michael Lawrence, standing in the doorway, staring at me and Jimmy. I wanted to wave, but my hands were full. Jimmy didn't notice him there, and when he said something funny and laughed, I had to kind of laugh too. But as I watched, Michael put his head down and quickly crossed the room to grab a sweater he'd left on his chair. Suddenly, I felt really, really bad, even though I hadn't done anything.

"Walk you to class?" offered Jimmy.

"Um . . ."

But Michael was gone.

"Sure. Thanks."

I didn't know what Michael had made of me and Jimmy having a long, lingering lunch together. But I did know that if the shoe was on the other foot, I would not have liked it one bit. A sickish feeling settled into my chest and stayed there for the rest of the day. I had to think of a way to reach out to Michael. But how? I couldn't exactly say, *Hey, I love you and I think you might like me, though you don't show it often. But today, with Jimmy? That was just work. Nothing to it. Now let's go out on a date, okay? And don't forget to wear something washed in Tide.*

Ugh.

That afternoon I couldn't bear to hang around the gym watching Hailey's practice while I waited for mine to begin. I decided to chill at the newspaper office for an hour, secretly hoping that I might catch a glimpse of Michael and at least have a reason to chat with him.

There was hardly anyone there when I went in. Jeff Perry, one of the paper's photographers (not to mention one of Michael's best friends), was scrolling through photos he'd taken of eighth graders to accompany my article.

After we said hi, I stood behind him and looked over his shoulder, offering my opinion on which photos I liked.

Mr. Trigg heard us talking and came out to say hello.

"How's the article shaping up, Ms. Martone?"

"Actually, it's really good so far," I said. I had to smile, thinking of Jimmy Becker.

Mr. Trigg was pleased. He rocked on his heels and flopped his trademark scarf over his shoulder. "Good, good. So you have some good material?"

"Yes. Cintra was really nice, but Jimmy was *amazing*!" I said enthusiastically. I looked to Jeff to include him in the conversation, and that was when I saw him giving me a funny look. Duh! I practically smacked my hand to my head. I had some quick thinking to do.

"I mean, you know, he's an actor, so he's very charming . . ." *Not good! Not good! Martone, correct course!* I yelled at myself. "And he's kind of . . ." I looked at Jeff, and he was sitting with his arms folded, smirking at me knowingly.

"What?" I said.

"Nothing," he said. Smirk, smirk.

I decided to un-include him from the conversation, so I turned my back on him. *Who cares what Jeff Perry thinks, anyway?*

"He's almost a professional, you know."

Mr. Trigg nodded. "It's nice when someone's willing to open up. Of course, this is a soft piece, so you don't need to do much digging. Just know for the future that you'll need to be on guard with subjects who seem charming and willing. You might not be getting all of the information you need. That's when you need to dig deep and ask the tough questions, also do background work to make sure what they're telling you is true."

I nodded, avoiding looking at Jeff. Maybe he'd gotten bored.

But no.

"Want to see some cute pictures of Jimmy-pooh?" he said.

"Oh, shush!" I scolded. Ever so briefly, I weighed

the idea of declaring my love for Michael Lawrence to Jeff and Mr. Trigg. But I quickly decided that would be a bad idea. Also, I didn't want such a sacred and important piece of information to be part of a conversation with Mr. Trigg, in the newspaper office, when we were talking about Jimmy Becker!

"Here he is!" teased Jeff.

I turned on my heel. "I do not like him! Anyway, I have to go."

Mr. Trigg was smiling in amusement. "Never a good idea to fall in love with your subject, Ms. Martone! Hard to be objective!"

"I told you, I *don't* like him!" I shouted. Then I stormed, red-faced and indignant, out of the office.

Futsal practice would have been much, much better after all.

Chapter 7

JOURNALIST FIRES BEST FRIEND, SEEKS NEW TALENT

★ ★ ★

I practically ran to the gym, just to get away from that stupid scene in the newspaper office. What a wasted trip: I hadn't checked for any new Know-It-All letters, I hadn't seen Michael, and I'd been falsely accused of having a crush on Jimmy Becker by a teacher and by Michael's best friend! *Falsely Accused Journalist Must Clear Own Name!*

Ugh!

Fuming, I slammed my messenger bag onto the bleachers and tried to take deep breaths to stop my heart from pounding.

Hailey was having a great time, running sprints, doing agility drills, laughing with her coach and her teammates. I guess this is what team membership provides: structure, health and fitness, a common goal, friendships. It did seem appealing.

After I calmed down a little, I thought about my Michael problem. I needed to see him more now that we weren't writing together, and I needed to let him know I liked him. Or, if not that I liked him, at least that I didn't like Jimmy. Or something!

What could I do?

I opened my notebook to brainstorm a little. Lists relax me. (Michael sometimes calls me "Listy" as a nickname. Or he used to, back when we were working together.) Here's what I came up with as ways to interact with ML:

1. Ask for his help/opinion on my article
2. Ask for help in training for tryouts
3. Confess that I am you-know-who for the paper
4. Ask for baking lessons

Number one didn't appeal to me because I didn't actually need his help.

Number two was a no-go. It's not like Michael is a gymnast anyway, and it would be complicated to mix him up in that, especially since I am already overstaffed in that department.

Number three would make me break a promise to Mr. Trigg. And while I might be willing to do that in the name of love, it would haunt me. And if it ever got out, I would definitely not make editor in chief next year.

Number four, though . . . that had potential.

Michael Lawrence makes the most delicious, melt-in-your-mouth cinnamon buns you've ever eaten. I've had them a couple of times, and they are insanely good. The downside of learning how to make them would be that he might not make them for me anymore, but the lesson time I'd spend with him would certainly offset that. Then, one day, when we're married, I'd announce that I quit baking and that he's in charge of it for good.

I chewed on my pen and tried to think of any other possibilities, short of asking Michael out. Soon Hailey's practice was over, and it was time for my training session.

"Yo," said Hailey, all flushed and happy.

"Yo," I said, all cranky.

"Yo?" Hailey was asking me what was wrong.

"Yo-yo," I said.

"What the heck? Speak English!" she said finally.

"Mr. Trigg and Jeff Perry think I like Jimmy Becker, and they're going to tell Michael!" I wailed.

"What?" Hailey was superconfused now, and I wasn't even speaking Yo.

I explained what had happened, and she shook her head slowly from side to side as we entered the gymnastics room and casually waved at Coach Lunetta.

"So now what?" she asked.

"I was thinking I need to reach out to him and show some interest," I offered.

"Bingo!" said Hailey, smacking her fist into her palm. "But how?" Her brow wrinkled in thought.

"Well, I've been working on that, too," I said. "I think I should ask him for a baking lesson—how to make those cinnamon buns."

"Genius!" declared Hailey. "But wait. That won't work! You can't be eating any of those right now while you're training. We'll need to think of something else."

"Hailey, I would eat fast food every day if it meant I might make headway with Michael Lawrence."

Hailey stared at me. "Really?" I nodded and she shook her head. "Then you're not serious about becoming an athlete. I should have known."

"First of all, you are the junk-food kid of all time," I said. "I have seen what you eat for lunch every day. And second of all, I just said I was considering this plan, not that I'm going to do it. And as for the cinnamon buns, it's not like I have to eat them. Anyway, one batch of cinnamon buns never ruined an athlete's career."

"Humph," said Hailey. "Just know that you are on parole as my trainee."

"Oh, whatever!"

During practice, I was distracted. Even as I did my routine, I kept craning my neck to see if I could spy Michael through the doorway, in the other gym. It was a little dangerous. Finally, Hailey said, "Do I have to shut this door to get you to focus?"

"No, no, sorry. I'm focused," I said. And I did try harder for a little while.

But as I was spinning around on the bars, I spied someone new out of the corner of my eye, standing in the doorway. I was moving so fast, I couldn't stop to see who it was, but I hoped it was Michael, of course.

I worked my hardest on the rest of the routine, did a really daring dismount, and stuck the finish like I was at the Olympic trials. I was so proud. Only when I heard clapping did I turn around to the doorway, a look of fake surprise on my face, with a smile.

Only it wasn't Michael.

It was Jenna Palmer.

"Great job, Sam!" she called.

"Hey, Jenna!" I hid my disappointment and crossed the room for a quick chat.

Hailey was staring at Jenna like she had three heads, probably jealous and territorial.

"Jenna, this is my friend Hailey Jones. Hailey, Jenna Palmer."

"Best friend," corrected Hailey.

Sighing, I rolled my eyes. ***Journalist Publicly***

Announces "Best" Friend.

"Nice to meet you," said Jenna. She was much nicer and more polite than Hailey.

"Are you here to practice for tryouts?" I asked. Might as well cut to the chase.

"Me? Oh no." Jenna blushed. "I'm just here to find out when they are. I thought I might come watch." She blushed even harder.

"You should try out!" I said, hoping to encourage her. Darn, I wish that Know-It-All letter could come out sooner. There just wouldn't be any time between the next issue of the paper and the start of tryouts.

"No, no," said Jenna, backing away with her palms in the air, as if trying to ward me off.

Just then Kristen Durkin came in with her little gym bag. She said a friendly hello to everyone and went to stretch on the exercise mat.

"She's on the team," I whispered, gesturing to Kristen. "And she's really nice. Come on! It'll be fun!"

"Really, I'm just an enthusiastic fan, not a participant. I promise. Anyway, I've got to go. I'll see you later! Nice to meet you!" she said to Hailey.

"Yeah," said Hailey grumpily.

After Jenna was out of earshot, I lit into Hailey. "What is wrong with you? Why were you so rude to her?"

"I wasn't rude! I just don't have the same desire that you have to go around inviting everyone to everything. If she tries out, it's one more person you are competing against for a spot on the team."

I folded my arms and narrowed my eyes at Hailey. "I hardly think asking one person to try out is a big deal."

"I'm just glad you didn't offer me to train her," said Hailey. "I thought that was coming next."

I smacked my forehead with my hand. "I should have thought of that! Of course! How can she train without a trainer?"

Hailey looked at Kristen across the room. "She is," said Hailey.

I followed her gaze. "Kristen? She's already on the team."

Hailey shook her head mildly. "I'm not so sure about that. I don't remember seeing her last year at any meets."

"Look, we're not talking about Kristen. I just

think . . . see, Jenna is new . . ." How was I going to explain all this to Hailey without admitting that I'm Dear Know-It-All and telling Hailey all about Jenna's letter? "And, anyway, maybe it's hard for her since she doesn't know that many people here, and maybe she doesn't have the courage. She just needs a friend to give her a boost. Like you're doing for me! Only she doesn't have anyone." I shrugged and held my hands out at my sides, palms up.

Hailey looked away. "So I'm a mean person just because I don't know who she is and I don't want her to train with us?"

I smiled. "Kind of!"

"Oh, whatever. Go get on that beam," ordered Hailey.

"Aye aye, Captain." I saluted and crossed over to the beam.

Knowing how good Kristen was on beam made me a little nervous to try it with her right there. I took a deep breath, shook out my arms and legs, closed my eyes to visualize a perfect routine (Hailey had read that advice on some website), and then I began. I felt badly that I had kind of chased Jenna off. At least I should have suggested she stay and watch. The thought distracted me, and I kept falling off the beam. I made a mental note to make it up to her by inviting her to have lunch with me and Hailey. That made me feel a little better. I glanced over at one point and saw Hailey and Kristen chatting. Phew. Seeing that Hailey was being nice to someone (and more importantly, that they weren't staring at me), I was able to relax a little.

After trying the beam for a while, I wanted to do something else. Something I was good at. In other words, the bars. But now Kristen was on them. I decided to take a break and went to check in with Hailey again.

Hailey tried to give me some advice on what I'd been doing wrong, but I knew it was Kristen whose advice I really needed. Or even Allie's, though I hated to admit it. I decided I'd better fill Hailey in.

"So Allie's feelings were supposedly hurt since I didn't ask her to train me," I said in an annoyed voice.

Hailey looked at me wide-eyed. "Is she mad at me?"

"No, don't worry. But my mom thinks I need to

butter her up and ask for her help."

"Why don't you invite her to come train with us?" Hailey asked hopefully.

"Oh, so *now* you're Miss Social, inviting people around."

Hailey scoffed. "Whatever. She was only the star of the team for three years. You'd be a fool not to use that resource. I thought of it before, but I figured she'd be too busy."

"I know." I nodded. She was right. I'd work up to it tonight.

Kristen was struggling on the bars, and I could see what she was doing wrong. She wasn't getting up enough speed before she tried her dismount. She repeated the exercise about three times. Finally, I had to say something.

I went over to the bars. "Hey, Kristen, please don't think I'm being pushy, because . . . obviously, you're amazing at gymnastics."

Kristen blushed, which I hadn't expected, and shrugged. "I can't figure this out. I stink at bars!" she said.

"Well, from across the room, what I'm seeing

is that you're not getting up enough speed to nail that dismount. I think you should either do one more spin before you try it or maybe just work on a different dismount that doesn't need so much momentum going into it, you know?"

Kristen looked like a lightbulb had gone on over her head. "Oh! Great idea! Do you mind watching while I try again?"

"Sure," I said, and I folded my arms and stood to watch. And, of course, she did the extra spin and nailed the dismount. Actually, she had a little too much speed going into it, so she couldn't stick the finish, but she basically got the routine right.

"Thanks!" she said.

I was happy my advice had worked. "No problem. Listen, do you have any advice for me on beam?"

"Sure!" she said, and she walked me over and gave me a few really great pointers. We split up and practiced a bit more, then I was ready to pack it in. I'd really made some progress today, and I was psyched. Plus, my endorphins were flying from all the exercise.

But then I reached Hailey by the door, and her endorphins had clearly worn off.

"I guess you don't need me anymore, now that you have that hotshot training partner. I was just coming to tell you I was leaving," she said grumpily.

"Oh, Hails, come on. I was just getting some pointers. You don't need to be mad. It was really helpful. And when we come back this weekend—*with Allie!*—I'll know what to work on."

"Right. This weekend. I was going to tell you, but I didn't want to hurt your feelings or anything, since things aren't going so well for you with Michael. But Danny Burke invited me to the movies on Saturday afternoon. So I can't come that day."

"What? You're kidding!" Millions of different emotions swarmed inside me. Shock at the news, first of all; then surprise and some disappointment that Hailey hadn't told me immediately; anger that she had withheld info from me, especially because she did it out of pity; and, of course, jealousy, because I'd loved Michael for so long and he'd never asked me out. But I also felt a little bit of disgust. Danny Burke! I mean, come *on*! Plus, I felt ditched. "Wow," I said calmly. "That's great. I'm surprised you didn't tell me sooner."

Hailey looked down at her fingernails and shrugged. "I can tell you don't like him," she said.

Uh-oh. Now I'd have to lie. "Well, I don't *like* him like him, of course. But for you . . . he's fine. I mean, he's great!" I crossed my toes inside my shoes as I lied to my best friend.

Hailey looked at me, unconvinced.

"I'm just . . . a little bummed that I'll have to train without you this weekend. That's all."

"Why don't you ask your new BFF over there? I'm sure she'd be eager to help."

I followed Hailey's gaze to Kristen, who was stretching. "She's already on the team. I'm sure she has better things to do than train me," I said.

"Actually, things aren't always what they seem. She's not on the team," said Hailey.

"What? No way! I was sure of it. How do you know?" I said, surprised.

"I asked," said Hailey. And she left.

Chapter 8

BAD CHOICES LEAVE REPORTER LONELY, LOVELESS, AND LUCKLESS

★ ★ ★

I couldn't let Hailey leave in a snit like that. I grabbed my stuff, yelled a hasty good-bye to Kristen and Coach Lunetta, and chased Hailey out of the gymnastics room.

Halfway through the basketball gym, I saw Michael. He was waiting on the sidelines to sub in to a scrimmage. Up ahead, Hailey was nearly out the door. What to do?

I wished I could magically clone myself. One of me would stay back in the gymnastics room with Kristen and find out why someone as good as her wasn't on the gymnastics team yet. My reporter's instinct just found that really odd. Then another me would chase Hailey down and make up. And a third me would go chat up Michael and let him know I was interested in him.

I took a deep breath. Well, the Kristen thing could wait, obviously. And between Michael and Hailey . . .

Michael looked up at me, and I smiled and raised my hand in a half wave. But he looked away, back at the game in front of him.

OMG! Was he mad at me? Had Jeff Perry gotten to him with the news (not!) that I liked Jimmy Becker? Or maybe he was just engrossed in the game. What should I do?

My feet continued to propel me forward. I guess they knew better than I did that I shouldn't let Hailey get away.

"Hey, Michael," I whispered as I passed behind him. But he didn't turn around. Had he not heard me?

Impulsively, I said it again, but louder.

This time he turned and kind of waved, but without a smile or anything. It was almost worse than him not reacting. I was mortified. I picked up my pace and hurried out the door, only to find Hailey gone.

I felt like the world's biggest loser. ***Bad Choices Leave Reporter Lonely, Loveless, and Luckless.***

That was me.

That night I sat on the floor on a little sheepskin rug in Allie's room and peppered her with questions about the balance beam until she finally sighed and said, "Look, do I have to come down there and show you myself?"

"Would you?" I asked desperately, as if that hadn't been my goal all along.

Allie made an aggravated sound like she had something caught in her throat. "Fine!" she said, but she tossed her hair, which is what she does when she feels proud, so I knew there was something else going on in that mind of hers.

"When? I mean, I know you're really busy," I said humbly.

Allie narrowed her eyes at me suspiciously. Maybe I was laying it on too thick.

"I am free Saturday morning from ten to twelve,"

she said, scrolling through her phone's calendar. That girl is totally wired. Nothing happens if it's not on her phone.

Maybe Hailey could make that, I thought. *If she ever answers my IMs.*

"Great!" I said with a big smile. "Thanks, Allie! You'll be a major help to me."

"Humph," said Allie.

Knowing I was ahead, I left. Although I did have a creeping feeling that Allie's help might not be exactly what I'd bargained for.

Back in my room, I decided to IM Hailey one more time.

Hey-lo Hail-o! Where r u? Allie coming Sat 10-12. Plz come!!!!

Then I sat and drummed my fingers on the desk. Nothing. Nothing. Nothing.

Finally, I sighed and opened up the document on my computer where I was transcribing my notes from my interviews with the eighth graders. Cintra's interview was all copied down, and I had some good quotes, and Jimmy's too, where I had some *great* quotes. I had an interview tomorrow morning during a free period with a popular girl named Toni Fox, and then another one at lunch, with a kind of nerdy kid named Walter something. I still hadn't scheduled Danny Burke yet. I knew I needed to, but I couldn't bring myself to contact him. And then there was the other person I couldn't bear to contact. Unrelated to the article, of course. The person who was leaving a major hole in my life.

Michael.

I knew what I needed to do, and I was trying to psych myself up. Maybe the best thing to do was *just do it,* like they say in the Nike ads. Fine! I tossed my hair, Allie-style, and dashed off a quick IM to Michael.

Hey stranger. I want to learn how to make yr amazing cinnamon buns. Baking lesson?

Then I pushed send before I could chicken out.

My heart pounded hard and my cheeks flushed deep red. I couldn't believe I'd done it! I tapped my foot anxiously while I waited to see if he'd reply. He was usually pretty fast at this time of night, since he was almost always at his computer. I went on

CNN.com to distract myself so I wouldn't get upset if I didn't hear from him right away. But rather quickly, I heard a beep. It was a message back!

My stomach lurched like I was on a roller coaster, and I clicked over to the message window with shaking hands. And there was his reply.

Recipe on sugar box.

Wait, what?

My palms went all clammy and I felt faint. Had Michael Lawrence just rejected me? I couldn't believe it! Was it really over, whatever we had, if we had actually ever had anything at all? OMG! In a panic, thoughts flashed through my head. Did he think I like Jimmy Becker? Had I ever even stood a chance with Michael? Was it really all business all along? I was mortified.

And Hailey still hadn't replied.

No friend, no boyfriend, no nothing. Right then all I wished was that I was an eighth grader who was graduating too. Like, immediately.

Writer Puts Past Behind Her, Sets Out on World Reporting Gig.

The next day at lunch, while I sat interviewing Walter Saunders about the chess club and that hilarious time in the lab when Tom Quinson accidentally spilled sulfur powder all over himself, I saw Michael arrive with Austin Carey. The two of them had their lunch trays and were looking around for a seat. The next thing I knew, they were sitting with Hailey and Kristen Durkin (!) and yukking it up, all of them having the time of their lives.

Humph! *See if Kristen Durkin likes your cinnamon buns, mister!* I wanted to yell. Instead, I steamed in silence.

Walter Saunders was perfectly nice, but it killed me to sit here with Walter while life went on at Michael's table without me. Walter was telling me how he wished he'd known there was an after-school robotics program, because he would have signed up for it in sixth grade, when suddenly he interrupted himself.

"I'm sorry. Is this really boring?" he asked after

he'd caught me staring at Michael and his group for the third time.

"What? No." I felt terrible and I decided to come clean. "I'm sorry I'm being rude, Walter. It's just . . . I'm in a fight with a friend of mine. Actually, my two . . . best friends. And I'm feeling really left out."

Walter was really great about it, and surprisingly enough, he had a much more mature take on middle school social life than most kids our age. He turned in his chair to see where I'd been looking. "Michael Lawrence?" he asked. I nodded miserably. "And who else?"

"Hailey Jones."

He thought for a minute, then he said, "You should just go over there. You know, so much in life gets made into a big deal because people don't do something immediately. You just can't let things continue to grow. It's like mold in the lab. The first day, it's little. The second day, still manageable. You can put a lid on it and it still seems fine. But by the third day, it is out of control, you know? And then it starts to smell."

I must've had a horrified look on my face because he laughed and apologized.

"All I mean is that you shouldn't let bad stuff grow. Clean it up fast, before it gets out of control and starts to ruin other stuff."

"Thanks. That's good advice. Nifty analogy, too," I said with a smile. Walter was a good guy.

I finished up the interview and decided to take Walter's advice. With my heart pounding, I crossed the room to Michael and Hailey's table.

"Hey," I said nervously.

"Hey, Sam!" said Kristen.

Hailey waved, but it wasn't exactly a warm greeting. I couldn't tell what it meant.

"Yo, Pasty," said Michael. Of course.

There was an empty seat, so I pulled it out and joined them.

"You know Austin, right?" asked Michael.

"Hi," we said to each other.

There was an awkward silence.

Oh no! I knew this was a terrible idea. I never should have come over here. Now I was mad at Walter. Why, oh why, was I taking advice from a nerd like him, anyway?!

"How's the article going?" I asked Michael and Austin.

They looked at each other. "Pretty good," they agreed, shrugging.

Hmm. Interesting that they didn't say "great." I wondered if it was easy work or if writing about finance wasn't turning out to be so exciting after all.

Then Michael reached into his backpack under the table and came up with a sheet of paper that he handed to me.

"Here," he said awkwardly. "I made a copy of the recipe for you."

I looked down at the paper in my hand. *Sweet Sweet Sinnamon Rolls*, it said.

"Thanks. I'm not sure mine will turn out as well as yours, though." I knew there was an opportunity here, but I didn't have the nerve to try again.

"You idiot!" interrupted Hailey. "Why don't you just show her how to make them?" she said to Michael. I loved Hailey right then. But I couldn't turn and smile at her to show my thanks.

Michael looked at me in surprise. "What? Why?"

"Maybe you have the best technique?" I said, thinking fast but shrugging to play it cool. "Maybe there are baking tricks you use that you don't realize?"

Michael looked dumbfounded. "Uh, okay. I could show you how . . ."

Bingo!

". . . that is, if you're not too busy with Jimmy Becker," he continued.

"What?" Infuriatingly, I turned bright red.

"See!" said Michael, wagging a finger at me. But he didn't look pleased. "I heard you two had something going on!"

"Absolutely not! I can't believe it. I can't even interview somebody for the school paper without being the target of gossip."

"Trust me, Lawrence," said Hailey. "She does not like that guy. I can guarantee it."

Thank you, Hailey, thank you, Hailey. I sent her my strongest ESP messages.

"Hmm. I don't know . . . ," Michael teased in a singsong voice.

"Please," I said, looking at him with my most level glare.

"Okay, fine. I believe you. I think," he said.

"Look, just teach me how to make the cinnamon buns, okay?" I said. I didn't want to lose the opportunity before we'd firmed up a plan.

"Okay, when?" said Michael.

And then, "Hello, people!" We were interrupted by Mr. Annoying himself: Danny Burke.

I looked at Hailey and saw that she had turned bright red. And so had Kristen! What was it with this guy? I felt Michael look at me, so I turned and looked at him, and when our eyes met, I rolled mine and shook my head a little. He looked relieved. Maybe he thought that I liked Danny too.

I turned back to hear what Danny was saying. "So I'll meet you there? For the three o'clock show, okay?"

And Hailey was nodding and beaming, ecstatic.

As soon as he was out of earshot, Kristen said, "Oh, Hailey, you are so lucky! I can't believe he asked you out!"

"Well, it's not really asking me out. We're just meeting at the movies," she said modestly, but I could tell she was thrilled. She looked at me, smiling, and I could do nothing but smile back. Great.

"Hails, uh . . . about that guy?" said Michael.

I whipped my head to look at Michael. Would he dare to discourage her? Did he have the nerve to do what I couldn't? It would be perfect if he did it, because if I did it, Hailey would think it was only because I was jealous.

"Yeah, he's great, isn't he? So funny," she said.

Michael looked pained. "Yeah. Right. Um, just . . . sometimes things aren't really what they seem, is all. Just . . . keep your eyes open, you know?"

Hailey fluffed her hair. "Whatever that means, Lawrence," she said, looking away to the side.

"I'm just looking out for you," he said, and I knew he was.

"I can look out for myself," said Hailey, staring him down.

That was mean. "Michael is just trying to be nice, Hails," I said.

She glared at me.

"Danny's nice!" Kristen piped up.

"Yeah, to *a lot* of people," said Michael, with heavy emphasis on "a lot."

"And . . . ," I said, not sure what to add.

Hailey started to stand up. "Yeah, well, maybe if people focused on their own love lives around here, they wouldn't be so busy meddling with other people's." She glared at me and Michael. I was embarrassed but tried to play it cool.

As Hailey stood there, I said in what I hoped was a neutral voice, "Maybe this isn't the time to discuss these sorts of things."

"I've gotta run," said Austin, picking up his tray to leave.

"Me too," agreed Kristen. "I'll walk with you."

As soon as they were far enough away, I said, "I guess those two are taking your advice, focusing on their own love lives." And the three of us wound up laughing for a happy moment. We'd reached an uneasy truce, for now, though I still didn't have a real baking date with Michael.

Baking Plans Fall Flat, Journalist Miserable.

Chapter 9

ROOKIE IMPRESSES THE PRO!

★ ★ ★

Michael had to run, and luckily, Hailey reminded him about our baking date one last time before he left. He promised to IM me later, and that was good enough for now.

As Hailey and I walked toward our fifth-period classes, we apologized to each other for being jerks, and then Hailey dropped the bombshell that Kristen wasn't even planning on trying out for the gymnastics team this year. She didn't think she was good enough and she wanted to keep taking gymnastics classes for one more year before going for it.

I couldn't believe this news. Kristen was certainly better than me, so if she wasn't trying out, why was I? Hmm. It looked like Kristen would also benefit from my reply to Jenna's Know-It-All letter. I'd write that tonight when I got home. The *Cherry Valley Voice* couldn't come out soon enough!

There was one more thing that needed addressing. "Hails, listen. Just be careful with Danny. I don't want to see you get your heart broken," I said before we parted ways outside the classroom doors.

"Why would you assume he'd break mine and not the other way around?" she asked.

"Have you seen his Buddybook page?" I asked.

"Yeah. So? He has a lot of friends," she said, shrugging.

All girls, I thought grimly.

"Right. Well, see you later," I said. "Are you coming to gymnastics tomorrow morning with me? Ally's coming, from ten to twelve."

"Maybe," said Hailey. "I'll try."

I couldn't imagine what else she had going on, especially if her date wasn't until three. "Okay, bye," I said.

"Bye," Hailey called over her shoulder.

"And good luck," I whispered under my breath.
Friend Ignores Repeated Warnings, Proceeds at Own Risk, I thought.

There was no word from Michael that night. I actually cried a little when I was going to sleep. I mean, this whole thing was so humiliating. Does he like me or not? I didn't know what to do. I slept fitfully, waking twice to check my computer for his IM, but no luck.

Ally and I were up early Saturday morning, and after she did her homework, we rode our bikes to my school to the open practice session in the gymnastics room. Still no word from Michael.

From the moment we walked in, of course, Coach Lunetta was fawning over Allie, making a huge deal of her, introducing her to the new junior coach as "our star," and all this other stuff that made me want to gag. But Allie was eating it up. The younger girls were glancing at her shyly, and some were openly staring at her, like she was a celebrity and they couldn't decide if they had the nerve to ask for her autograph. Needless to say, it was a little while before we got down to business.

"Okay, show me what you've got," said Allie.

I started on the uneven bars because I wanted Allie to take me seriously. I knew if I started on one of my weaker areas, she'd be condescending and bossy and I wouldn't be able to shake her bad attitude.

After I did my sample routine, I stuck the finish and Allie clapped. I knew she was surprised and impressed. I flushed with pride.

"Wow. I'm not sure why you need me here," she said. "That was pretty sweet. I had no idea you knew how to do that."

Rookie Impresses the Pro!

I shrugged modestly. "Well, the uneven bars have always been my strongest suit."

"Nice. I have some critiques, of course . . ."

Of course, I thought.

". . . but let's save them all until the end so we don't lose momentum."

"Okay. So, vault, then."

We went through the different apparatuses one by one. My floor routine was very weak (I stink at all those handsprings and somersaults and stuff, not to mention my clumsy feet), and when we finally got to the beam, the balance of power had definitely shifted. Allie was back to her usual queen-bee bossiness and had decided *not* to hold back her critiques—there were simply too many to keep track of, she told me, and she'd never remember them all, so she'd just have to call it as she saw it.

Right as she was about to light into me about my balance beam routine, Hailey appeared, thank goodness.

"Hey, Allie!" she said.

"Hailey! What's up?" They greeted each other happily, and I rolled my eyes.

While they filled each other in, I noticed that Kristen and Jenna had both arrived. Kristen was working on the vault while Jenna stood by the sidelines. Yay! Maybe this meant they were still thinking about trying out!

I turned to Allie. "Check this out," I said. "See

the girl in the red leotard? Watch how good she is." We all three stood and watched as Kristen sailed though her vault, nailing a roundoff into a somersault as she flew over the table.

"Wow," said Allie. "She's like me in the olden days."

I felt a twinge of jealousy right then, knowing it was true and wishing Allie had said it about me instead. But I went for the clincher. "But get this. She doesn't think she's good enough to try out!"

Hailey nodded solemnly at Allie's shock.

"And see the girl in the yellow sweats hanging around by the door? She wants to try out too, but she's too scared."

Hailey looked at me in confusion. "She does? How do you know that?"

Secret Agent Blows Cover, Nearly Spoils Mission!

"Oh. What?" I stuttered. I tried to think fast to come up with a reason. "Oh, just . . . you know. From around."

"Because I heard her saying she's just a fan," Hailey said. "That she has no interest in trying out."

"Oh, well. Um, sometimes people say one thing and mean another. You know, like what was that thing Michael said? Things aren't always what they seem."

Hailey gave me a hard look and turned back to Allie.

"So what are you up to this weekend?" asked Allie.

Hailey blushed. "Actually . . . I have a date," she said shyly.

Allie exploded. "Hailey! That's awesome! Wow! Who's the lucky dude? Where are you going?"

Hailey explained everything while I stood there, biting my tongue and wishing we could just work on my routine. This whole Danny Burke thing was awkward for me.

"So what are you going to wear?" asked Allie, getting down to brass tacks.

Hailey looked at Allie hopefully. "Uh, that's kind of why I came this morning. I wanted some advice."

Oh, so *that's* why she came. *Why is everyone in my life so aggravating? It's time for some new friends,* I thought spitefully.

"You know what, guys? I'm just going to go talk to Jenna for a minute." I crossed the room and found Jenna chatting with Coach Lunetta, using all sorts of technical terms. *See, Hailey?* I wanted to yell. *She* does *want it!*

"Hey, Jenna!" I said.

"Hi, Sam!" Jenna was definitely happy to see me.

"Are you here to practice?" I asked.

Jenna laughed. "No, I'm not trying out! I told you, I'm just a fan."

I gave her a knowing look. "Okay, but whenever you're ready, I am happy to train with you. Just say the word."

"Thanks," she said. "So what's new? Any big weekend plans?"

"Nah," I said, thinking of my nonexistent baking date with Michael. I was hoping against hope that when I got home from training, there'd be a message from him.

"How are things with Michael Lawrence?" Jenna asked with a smile.

In shock, I turned to her. "What? But how did you know . . . ?" I spluttered.

Jenna laughed. "I may be shy, but I'm not blind! One advantage of being the new kid is that you are kind of invisible, so you really get to observe. I can just tell you like him by the way your face lights up whenever you see him."

I beamed. "I really do like him. I just wonder why he doesn't notice."

"Boys are dense," she said. "But I'm sure he'll come around."

"Any boy plans in your future?" I asked in a gently teasing voice. I knew there weren't, because she was so new and everything.

But Jenna blushed. "Actually, I have a movie date tomorrow."

"That's great! Someone from here?" I asked, racking my brains for anyone suitable.

Jenna nodded. "Yeah! Danny Burke," she said.

My jaw must've dropped, but I was speechless.

"I know," she said, modest but obviously proud. "I couldn't believe it either when he asked."

"Wow," I said, shaking my head. My heart was racing with anger. Should I tell Jenna? Hailey? What to do? "That's, um . . . what are you going to see?"

Jenna named a movie, and at least it wasn't the one Hailey was going to see with him today. That would have just been too much.

"Well, I want to hear all about it next week. You should sit with us at lunch on Monday," I said. In the meantime, I vowed to get in touch with Mr. Burke himself. My interview request was long overdue. Maybe I'd just rake him over the coals face-to-face, while taking notes. Let's see how he'd like that!

"Okay! See you then!" said Jenna, obviously psyched to have a friend.

Watch out, Mr. Burke, I thought. *Because Sam Martone, aka Super Friend, is coming to get you. And she is out for revenge!*

I crossed back over to Allie and Hailey, biting my tongue to keep from saying anything. I wouldn't even be able to tell Allie later, because I knew Hailey would be mortified if Allie knew.

"All right, ladies, let's get down to business," I said. If we could just focus on the routines, I'd be in good shape.

"Great," said Allie, rubbing her palms together in kind of an evil way.

Oh no, I thought. *Now what?*

Then I tripped on the vault mat and had to sit for a few minutes until the pain in my foot subsided.

To her credit, Allie helped me a lot. She gave me a bunch of ideas (easy tricks that looked hard) and tips, and she gave Hailey some pointers of things for us to work on next week before tryouts. I had to hug her at the end because she really was helpful.

I hugged Hailey, too, when we parted, even though Hailey is not much of a hugger.

"Good luck. Have fun!" I said, and she nodded. I knew she was nervous. I just hoped it went well and that Danny didn't break her heart. (I knew she wouldn't be breaking his. How can your heart break when you have so many other hearts waiting in the wings for it?)

At home I marched up the stairs to e-mail Danny Burke to set up our interview. I looked forward to phrasing it in the most businesslike manner so there wouldn't be any confusion as to why I was contacting him. In my anger, I had momentarily forgotten I was waiting to hear from Michael, so imagine my surprise when I found an IM from him waiting.

Pasty, sorry for delay. Finally got everyone to clear out for a couple hours tomorrow. R u free from 2-4? LMK. Thx.

Aha! So that was it! He didn't want anyone snooping around while we were baking! That was a good sign. Smiling, I sat in my swivel chair and spun from side to side happily. *Good things come to those who wait*, I told myself. And I didn't even spin myself out of my chair.

And now for Danny Burke!

In honor of Danny, I cracked my knuckles and rolled up my sleeves, then I began to type. It took a little while to get the wording right, but I was pretty satisfied with the end product.

Danny,

The *Cherry Valley Voice* has requested I interview you for an upcoming article on eighth graders' experiences at the school. I *know* how busy you are, but if you are willing to participate, please reply to me with at least three time slots when you would be available for an interview.

Thank you,

Samantha Martone

I squinted and considered not italicizing the word "know," but I decided I'd let him wonder what I meant by that. It would keep him on his toes. I couldn't wait to come up with some questions for Mr. Lover Boy that would really call him out.

Since I was on a roll, I took out the Dear Know-It-All letter from Jenna and gave it another read. Then, picturing her happy face at the gym, I settled into writing what turned out to be a very inspiring response, if I do say so myself. I thought a lot about my interviews with the eighth graders and how they focused on doing things now so you didn't regret not trying later. I even used *carpe diem*, which was a big Mr. Trigg phrase; it means "seize the day" in Latin. I knew he'd like it. Then I sent it off to Mr. Trigg by e-mail for his review.

That night I must've checked my computer a dozen times, hoping for word from Hailey. Either it had gone great or gone terribly, but she wasn't saying. I didn't want to IM her because I didn't want to put her on the spot, but it was agony to be kept in suspense.

Even Allie poked her head in once, to check. "Any word from Hailey?" she asked.

"Uh-uh," I replied.

"Hmm," said Allie. And she shut the door.

Well, I thought, turning off my computer that night and getting ready to climb into my bed with a book, *whatever happened happened.* I just hoped Hailey was okay.

Despite Warnings and Advice, Friend Must Go It Alone.

I couldn't say I wished the same for myself.

Chapter 10

JOURNALIST AIMS TO BE VOICE OF REASON

★ ★ ★

I finally bit the bullet and called Hailey at ten on Sunday morning.

"Hey!" I said, all casual. "What's up?"

"Not much," said Hailey. "What are you doing today?"

I debated telling her about my baking plans with Michael, not knowing how yesterday had gone for her. But I could hardly lie. "Actually, Michael finally invited me over to bake! Woo-hoo!"

She laughed. "Yay! Just don't eat too many buns. We've got gymnastics to practice tomorrow, and you need to feel your best."

"Right. As if I'm making the team anyway," I said. I'd committed to trying out after Allie put all that time into my practice yesterday. Hailey's disappointment I could deal with; she was used to me bagging out on athletic stuff. But Allie would never let me live it down if I'd wasted her time.

"Okay, Hails, you're killing me. How did it go yesterday?"

There was a pause. "Um, actually, it was really fun. I liked the movie."

"Yeah, yeah, but what about Danny? Was he nice? Did you guys talk?"

"Well, it was kind of awkward at first. But once the movie started, we laughed and stuff. Then after, we talked for a minute and our moms came to get us so it was kind of over."

"Huh." It sounded like kind of a letdown. But maybe that's what all dates were like.

"Yeah."

We were quiet for a minute. "So do you like him?" I asked.

"I don't know," admitted Hailey.

"Do you think he likes you?"

"I think he likes a lot of people," said Hailey.

Finally! This was heading in the right direction.

"Why do you think that?" I asked, all innocent.

"Well, because while we were waiting to go in, we played a couple of video games in the lobby, and he kind of flirted with a lot of girls around."

"Oh. That's annoying."

"Yeah. So . . ."

Hailey sounded sad. I didn't know what to say.

"Well . . . ," I said.

"Anyway, it's pretty cool that you're going to Michael's later!" Hailey is such a good friend. She sounded happy for me for real.

"Yeah." I smiled. "I'll let you know how it goes."

"Yeah, don't keep me waiting," she joked.

"Ahem!"

And we laughed.

Later that afternoon I almost ended up being late for my baking date, which would not have been good.

Allie got wind of my plans and decided she needed to curl my hair with a curling iron. But she went overboard and I wound up looking like a baby doll with ringlets, so I had to wash my hair, which meant I needed to change my outfit (which I had already changed five times). I finally settled on a high ponytail, a fitted gray turtleneck, my pearl-colored cords with a black belt, and chunky ankle boots of Allie's that I borrowed (and were slightly too large).

Anyway, I clomped over to Michael's, breathless, and just made it by 2:05.

The Lawrence house is nice. It's painted white with dark shutters on a really pretty street. When I arrived, his parents were still there.

His dad opened the door, and Michael came skidding out to greet me, sliding on his socks in the front hall. His dad looked just like him, only with salt-and-pepper hair and some wrinkles when he smiled. He was friendly to me and teased Michael about his new cooking school.

In the kitchen I said hi to his mom, whom I'd met before. She's very pretty and also friendly—older than my mom, but then Michael has two older brothers. His mom had a big basket of clean laundry she was carrying upstairs. "Sports clothes," she said, rolling her eyes and laughing.

"What a surprise!" I said.

Michael was nervous, I could tell. So was I. I almost wished his parents would stay and hang out in the kitchen with us. I could talk to grown-ups all day, but leave me alone with a cute boy and no actual article to write and I get tongue-tied.

"Offer Sam something to drink," called his mother as she left the room.

"So . . . can I get you something to drink?" he asked.

I wasn't really thirsty, but I remembered how grateful I'd been when Michael had been over at my house and had said yes to a drink. It gave me something to do, getting it, and it calmed us both down a lot.

"Sure," I said, thinking of all that in a flash.

Michael grinned. "Great!" He flung open the fridge. "We have Gatorade, Powerade, protein smoothies, fortified coconut water—"

"Ugh! I think I'll skip the jock juice and just go with plain water, please."

"Smart choice," said Michael, and while he

busied himself getting it, I looked around. Michael had laid out all of the ingredients and the tools we'd need. I was impressed with his organization skills. The oven was preheated, the butter was soft. It looked like he'd been ready for a while.

"So, what's up with your article?" I asked, making conversation.

"It's okay. But it turns out high finance is not as juicy as we'd hoped," he said.

I studied his face to see if he'd give more away.

"Is Austin nice?" I asked. I knew I was fishing, but I wanted a little more feedback than I was getting.

"Yeah. He's cool. He's a great writer," said Michael, handing me a glass of ice water.

I flinched. Was Austin a better writer than me? I couldn't actually ask. That would really be fishing.

"Cool," I said, taking a sip of my water.

"It's not the same as working with you." Michael shrugged casually.

I raised one eyebrow. "Oh yeah? Is that a good thing or a bad thing?" I teased, dreading one answer and hoping for the other.

Michael looked up and smiled. "It's just different."

Hmm. Okay. It was obvious he wasn't going to give me any more information. Time to change the subject.

"All right, so how do you make your world-famous cinnamon buns?" I asked, hopping up on a stool at the counter.

"First we wash our hands," said Michael with a smile.

I jumped down to follow suit and then let myself me guided through the entire step-by-step recipe. It wasn't that hard after all, and I think Michael liked being the teacher and me being the student. Usually, we're sort of competitive with each other. It was nice to just relax around each other. Also, I didn't drop anything or trip or fall or do anything klutzy!

Novice Holds It Together in Company of Pro!

When the cinnamon buns were baking and we were whisking the sugar icing, talk turned to Danny Burke.

"That guy is too much," said Michael.

"I know!" I agreed.

"I think he's probably pretty nice, but his whole 'ladies' man' thing is really annoying. I wonder what he was like at his old school."

"I'm tempted to do some digging and find out. You remember I have to interview him for my article?"

"Right! I forgot! When?"

"I'm not sure yet. Soon," I said. "I can't wait to grill him. Did you know he asked Hailey to the movies yesterday and Jenna today?"

"Gross," said Michael.

"He must have some kind of a weird complex," I said. "And I wish I could tell Hailey and Jenna about each other, but I don't dare."

Michael looked at me. "You can't. You've just got to let them find out on their own."

I nodded miserably. "I just hate keeping secrets from my friends." I sighed, thinking how I was keeping my job as Know-It-All a secret from Michael.

We talked about a lot of things—school, news,

journalism, sports—and it was really fun. Michael gave me a few tips on making the buns, and although I had gone through all the motions, I was pretty distracted. I'm not sure I could reproduce the same results in my own kitchen.

At the end, we frosted the buns, and once they'd cooled a little, we sat down to have some with a glass of milk.

"Oooh, Hailey would kill me if she could see me right now," I said, grinning guiltily.

"Why?" Michael looked confused.

"Eating a cinnamon bun while I'm supposed to be in training for gymnastics," I said. "Oh well!"

"I wouldn't worry. I'm sure you've got enough talent that one little cinnamon bun won't kill you."

"Thanks," I said. "So exactly how many little cinnamon buns *will* kill me?" I asked, greedily eyeing the plate with a smile.

When it was time to leave, I was bummed. But we both had homework, and Michael seemed to want me out of there before his brothers got home. I could relate. He wanted to walk me home. I said he didn't have to, but I was hoping he would. He insisted anyway, and I was really psyched. I had a little doggy bag of cinnamon buns in my hand, and we talked the whole way.

When we reached my gate, Michael put his hands in his pockets.

"Well, thanks!" I said. "Sorry I had to beat your door down for the baking lesson. I just didn't want to have to rely on you for my cinnamon bun needs." I was nervous. Was I supposed to hug him good-bye or something? We had fun together, but maybe he didn't like me that way.

"You can always count on me, Pasty," said Michael.

Now I was grinning from ear to ear. "Thanks. Ditto," I said. "Well. Bye!"

Michael was grinning too. "Bye!" he said, and I turned and fled up my driveway. When I got to the door, I turned back and he was still there. I waved happily and he waved back, and then he set off back to his house.

What a great afternoon!

Inside, I flung off my coat and ran upstairs. I had to tell someone all about my amazing time with

Michael. But at the top of the stairs, I hesitated. I'd been about to IM Hailey, but I suddenly realized it wouldn't be fair to gush on and on about how great my time with Michael had been when hers with Danny hadn't been the best. Hmm. Maybe Allie.

I knocked on her door but it turned out she wasn't home. Disappointed, I went into my room and checked my IMs anyway. There was one from Hailey asking how it went (that was nice) and one from Mr. Trigg saying he loved my Dear Know-It-All response letter (yay!). And I had an e-mail from Danny Burke:

Hey, Sammy. Can do first free tomorrow or lunch, or Tues first free. I'm lovin' that I'm tabloid material! See ya! DB

Sammy? I thought I might puke. And worse, I didn't have first free period available either day, so it would have to be lunch tomorrow. I gulped and typed back.

Danny, see you at lunch tomorrow. Thanks. Samantha.

I shuddered and sat still, debating whether to call Hailey. Then my IM beeped.

How was it????

I smiled and typed back.

Great! Thanks. Will call u later.

I couldn't call Hailey now. I decided to wait until I calmed down a bit. In the meantime, I plotted out my article. I could just slot Danny's material into it tomorrow night when I got home and submit the article first thing Tuesday.

Scanning through my notes and quotes, I realized there was a theme: *I wish*. Every eighth grader had said they wished they'd done something, whether it was Cintra wishing she hadn't been so shy in the beginning, or Jimmy wishing he'd tried out for plays sooner, or Walter wishing he'd known about the robotics class. I knew I needed to write an article that encouraged people to go for it, to try everything, work hard, be outgoing, take risks, and make the most of their time at Cherry Valley Middle School. Kind of like my letter to Jenna. That would be easy.

But I also felt bad for these kids with a whole bunch of regrets. Middle school is kind of a process—it's not like you can know everything about the place the first day you arrive. You also don't know everything about yourself the first day you arrive. Like, maybe Jimmy Becker wasn't even interested in theater when he got here. Maybe it came later, after his parents took him to see a play in the city. I didn't want people to be too hard on themselves. We're still kids and we can't do everything perfectly, right?

Sam Martone: *The Voice of Reason.*

I did a draft of my opening and closing paragraphs before saving the document and giving myself a chance to cruise around the news sites online. I always like to read good journalism while I'm working on a piece because it keeps my writing fresh and tight. It's also inspiring.

Finally, after all the work, my adrenaline had calmed down and I called Hailey to tell her about my baking session with Michael. There was one little detail irritating me, though, through our whole conversation, and that was my lunch plan for the next day with Danny Burke. Should I tell Hailey? Should I not? I wasn't sure.

Ultimately, I took my own advice from the

article and went for it.

"Hails, by the way, I have to have lunch with Danny tomorrow," I said quietly, and I bit my lip, waiting for her reply.

There was a silence for a few moments until Hailey said, "Why?"

"I have to interview him for the paper," I said. "You know how I've been interviewing eighth graders for the article on their memories of Cherry Valley? Well, Susannah wants to include Danny because he was new this year. She thinks he'll have an interesting perspective."

"Oh," said Hailey.

"Do you mind?" I asked, wincing.

"No, it's fine. Have fun," she said, but not that enthusiastically.

"Thanks," I said. "It's work, though, so I don't think it will be that fun."

"Yeah, well . . ."

Was I reading into it too much, or was Hailey down in the dumps? I didn't want to make a big deal about it, but I felt like I was leaving things unsettled.

"Okay . . . see you tomorrow. Call me if anything comes up."

"Bye."

After I hung up, I stared into space for a while. Things with Michael were always up in the air, and that was annoying, but at least I knew who I liked and I had a goal. Hailey was always kind of all over the place.

On the other hand, was liking only one boy pathetic? Why didn't I like more people? Hailey has already liked three different boys this year and it's only winter.

Sighing, I stood up and went to watch TV. Sometimes it's best to take a break and just clear your head.

Chapter 11

JOURNO SLEUTH NAILS IT AGAIN!

Danny Burke is not quite the person I thought he was, as it turns out.

Or, actually, he is the person I thought he was, but he actually has a pretty good reason for being that way. Not that I in any way approve, but at least I now understand.

Our lunch started annoyingly enough, as I had expected it would.

"Sammy!" he said, smiling his charming smile and indicating with his tray that I should follow him.

Walking in his wake as he called out to all the girls, I thought I'd puke. Girls were blushing, smiling, waving, and he was eating it up. When we sat and started to talk, it was all about this girl and that girl and so on.

Finally, I couldn't take it anymore. "Danny, why are you always trying to charm all the girls? You're kind of leading them all on, and it's mean!" My blood was starting to boil, and I was out to avenge his two-timing of Jenna and Hailey.

He looked at me in surprise. Was it because I'd asked such a blunt question or because I was clearly immune to his charms? But it was neither.

"What do you mean leading people on?" he asked.

"Well, you ask one girl to the movies one day and another to the movies the next day. You're texting this one and winking at that one. They all think you like them, and you're not really following through with any of them, so that's leading people on."

There! I'd said it! I sat back and waited for his answer.

But Danny had gone quiet. And serious. I'd never actually seen him not in charm mode. "Is that really what I do?" he asked in all sincerity. "Is that what people think?"

"Duh! Hello?"

"Wow," he said quietly. "I never saw it that way."

"What? You have to be kidding me! You're the class Romeo!"

"Huh."

"Isn't it on purpose?" I asked.

Danny shook his head. "No. Not at all. I mean, I wasn't trying to . . . I didn't mean to be dating different girls. I just thought I was making friends."

"Seriously? Asking girls to the movies, one after the other?"

He shrugged. "I haven't made any guy friends since I moved here last summer. I'm not on any sports teams, and I'm not in any hobby clubs or anything. When my mom died last spring, my dad moved us here to be closer to his sister's family so she could help out while he traveled for work. He's a salesman, so he's on the road a lot."

Ah, that's where all the flirty stuff comes from, I realized. The winking and compliments and everything a salesman knows how to do.

Journo Sleuth Nails It Again!

"Do you have any brothers or sisters?" I asked.

"I have two half sisters, but they're much older. They just think of me more as this cute little kid than a brother." He smiled kind of sadly and shrugged again. Suddenly, I was worried he might cry.

"So you're alone a lot or with your aunt?"

He nodded and took a sip of juice.

"Hmm." He must be pretty lonely, but I didn't want to make it worse by saying so. And now I could hardly go through the questions on my list about regrets and wishes. It would probably be easy to guess what Danny Burke wished. "Is that why you like the movies so much?"

"Yeah!" Here Danny perked up, and we moved on to a whole new discussion about Hollywood and everything.

"You know," I said, thinking, "it's not too late to join the film club. They do cool stuff. I'd join it if I had the time, but I just don't. They see a movie every week, and then they meet to talk about it. Usually, one of the members writes movie reviews for the paper."

"Really? I wish I'd known about that sooner," he said. "I'll check it out."

I love when people take my advice (obviously), so now I was liking Danny Burke a little more. I also felt sorry for him, which always makes it tough to hate someone. Anyway, once he calmed down the whole flirty act, he was actually a pretty decent guy. I thought about Michael's comment that "people aren't always what they seem." Now I thought that was even truer. I'd thought Danny was a sleazy jerk out to date all these girls. Now I could see that he was a lonely guy, scared and unsure of how to make friends with other guys, crazy about movies, so he imitates cheesy movie and TV stars and invites girls out and they think it's a date. Maybe it kind of is, but he doesn't mean it that way. I don't know if I could ever really be friends with him, unless he toned down his whole act a lot, but I felt like I understood him better now.

I spied Hailey across the room, and when she caught my eye, I waved her over to join us. She shook her head no, but when Danny turned, he waved her over too, and she finally stood up with her tray and joined us.

"I didn't know Mr. Burke here was such a

movie nut!" I said as Hailey sat down shyly.

She nodded. "Yeah. He knows a lot about movies and even filmmaking," she agreed.

Danny smiled, about to turn on the charm, but then he glanced at me and dialed it back. "Thanks, Hailey," he said.

I scolded myself for judging Danny before I'd really ever had a conversation with him. It was bad journalism. I made a mental note to try to remain objective before every interview. It would be hard, but it was important. Because once you have an impression of someone—right or wrong—it can be hard to shake.

Journo Has Long Way to Go.

I wrapped up the interview and had to dash to my next class. I left Hailey and Danny trailing behind, but this time I wasn't nervous about Hailey's heart getting broken. Danny probably wasn't the right guy for her, but at least he wasn't the jerk I'd thought he was, and that was a relief.

I ran into Jenna that afternoon, and she gave a similar account of her date with Danny. She was disappointed, and I listened sympathetically.

But whereas a few days ago I would have ranted about Danny, now I kind of gently shared the info about his dead mother and his loneliness ("Things aren't always what they seem . . ."). As I talked, I could see Jenna's sympathy grow and her disappointment lessen.

"I think what he really needs is a good friend," I said.

"I know the feeling," agreed Jenna.

"Well, you have at least one!" I said cheerfully.

"Thanks, I know," said Jenna, smiling.

Do-Gooder Advice Columnist Cheers the World, One Person at a Time!

By Wednesday I was down to my final practice before tryouts started on Friday after school. The gymnastics room was really crowded, with all the interested girls there at once, even the existing team members, polishing their routines. It was slow-going to get a turn on each apparatus, so I had to make the most of my time. Allie, Hailey, and Kristen were all there to help me, and Jenna came to watch too (still not motivated to try out herself, but I was sure that when my column came out on Friday, she'd get pumped and just go for it).

It was late when we were finally leaving, and I was so grateful to Allie and Hailey for devoting their whole afternoon to this that I promised to make them cinnamon buns over the weekend.

We said good-bye to Jenna, and I went to wish Kristen luck too.

"Oh, I'm . . . I don't think I'm going to do it," she said. "I just can't seem to get the bars right."

"Kristen, that's ridiculous! You have to try out! You're amazing! Who cares if bars aren't your best thing?"

She looked kind of sad. "I just . . . I don't know."

"I will see you here Friday afternoon. Do not skip it!" I commanded.

Kristen smiled. "I'll try," she said.

"Don't try. Do!" I said, laughing. That was a Haileyism.

Hailey's mom was outside in her car and offered to drive me and Allie home, but we wanted to walk since it was only five blocks, and

Hailey my trainer approved of the extra exercise. Walking home in the dark after all that workout time together, I felt close to Allie, so I filled her in on all the Michael Lawrence stuff and even a little of the Danny Burke stuff.

"So things aren't always what they seem, you know?" I said, trying out my new observation.

"Yeah," Allie agreed. "That's for sure," she said with a sigh.

"What do you mean?"

"Oh, nothing. Just . . . I always thought I'd be this gymnastics champ, and I'd be on the track for the Junior Olympics, and now look at us. I'm all washed up, and you're going to be the new champ."

"Hardly," I said, but inside I was thrilled at the compliment even as I knew it was a major exaggeration.

"Well, I just wish—" Allie stopped.

"What?" I asked.

"I wish I hadn't quit. I wish I'd stuck with it and worked harder."

I thought of my article. I guess everyone has regrets, no matter what age they are. But it seemed sad to hear Allie feeling all washed up in her teens.

"Listen, you made good choices. The gymnastics team was taking over your life. It was unhealthy. And when you stopped"—I didn't want to use the word "quit"—"it opened up room for a lot of other good things, like the website you run and your schoolwork and stuff."

"Hmm, I don't know," said Allie.

"Come on!" I said, wanting her to cheer up. "And you're superpopular!"

Allie smiled. "I know."

"And you're a great dancer and beautiful and smart and funny and . . ."

Allie smiled. "All right, now you're going overboard."

"Good, because I was running out of compliments. Now let's make some popcorn and watch some bad TV."

Allie laughed. "Sounds like a plan!"

I was glad I was able to snap her out of her sad mood.

★   ★   ★

So I didn't make the gymnastics team. That's what happened.

I went to the tryouts Friday after school. Allie came to watch when she got out of school, and Hailey skipped futsal (unprecedented!) to attend.

And you will never believe this, but Jenna tried out too! And so did Kristen.

What happened was the Dear Know-It-All letter came out in the paper earlier that day, and it was pretty darn good. Everyone was talking about it in the cafeteria, and when I got there, Hailey, Jenna, and Kristen were all milling around looking for a place to sit. I corralled them all and we sat together, which was really fun.

Here's the response I had written:

Dear Gymnastics Team Hopeful,

I am just going to tell you flat out—you should try out for the team. There are so many things we can change in our lives, but there is one thing nobody can do. And that is turn back time. Don't do (or in this case, *not* do) something you'll regret later. You don't want to spend the rest of your life wondering "what if." Just practice and then try your best. And let's just imagine for a minute that the worst happens—you *don't* make the team. So what? You're not any worse off than you are right now. Nothing has changed. So it's actually a can't-lose situation. You either make the team or you can sleep easy knowing you gave it your best shot. I have my fingers crossed for you. Good luck and *carpe diem*! That means "seize the day." Go for it!

Best wishes,

Dear Know-It-All

Jenna had a copy of the paper, and when she sat down, she said, "Hey, Sam! Did you see Dear Know-It-All? You wrote that, didn't you?"

I was so caught off guard that I blushed bright red. "What?" I said.

"I knew it!" cried Jenna. "I knew you wrote that letter in to the paper! Busted!"

It took another second for me to realize that she thought I was Gymnastics Team Hopeful, not Dear Know-It-All. Phew!

"Oh . . . no," I said, laughing. "That wasn't me. But it could have been!" In relief, I began eating my egg salad sandwich. But wait. How could she think it was me who wrote it if it was *she* who wrote it?

"Come on, fess up!" she pressed me. Was she just trying to throw people off her trail or what? I was confused.

"Wait, did you write it?" I asked.

But just then Kristen said softly, "Actually, it was me. I wrote the letter to Dear Know-It-All."

"What?" I whipped my head to the side to stare at her in shock. "Are you kidding?"

Kristen was the one to blush now. She shook her head and looked down at her plate.

"So it wasn't you?" I asked Jenna.

"No! And I thought it was you! But it was her!" Jenna laughed. "Well, it had to be somebody at this table, didn't it?"

"Not me!" said Hailey, happily eating a piece of cake.

"Wow. Good for you, Kristen! That was brave of you to write in. So you're going to go for it, right? Just like Dear Old What's His Face said?" I messed up the column name on purpose, just to throw them off my trail, in case I had acted suspicious.

"It's Dear Know-It-All," corrected Hailey in a snotty voice.

"Thanks," I said dryly. "How would I ever get by without you?"

Just then Danny Burke walked up. "Ladies, ladies, please! No fighting! There's enough of me to go around!"

Though he was being his usual flirty self, I had to laugh this time, and then he actually toned it down. "Anyone want to go to the movies with me this weekend?" he asked.

It was kind of a weird offer, throwing it out like that. I decided to call him on it.

"What are we supposed to do, Danny? Fight over your offer like a pack of dogs with a bone?"

He took it well, laughing. "As friends! I want to see that new scary movie that just came out in 3-D, and I hate going to the movies alone."

Hailey shrugged. "I might be able to go," she said.

"Me too," said Jenna.

"You know I joined the film club," Danny said, smiling at me. "So now I can get us discount tickets. Anyone else interested?"

Kristen couldn't go, and this was the last thing I wanted to get mixed up in, so we just let them plan their double not-date.

"Hey, I liked the article, by the way," said Danny. "I think the photos were pretty good too, right? I've, um . . . heard from a lot of . . . people that it's a good shot of me. I don't know." Danny was definitely letting up on the swagger, and I had to give myself a little credit for that.

"Thanks. I think it went over pretty well."

Mr. Trigg had loved it, even as he promised me a harder-hitting article for the next issue.

"And I'd like to write it with Michael," I had told him. I didn't want to live a life of regrets, wishing I'd gone for things that I hadn't.

Mr. Trigg had laughed. "Of course. The new Woodward and Bernstein," he added with a wink, referencing the famous journalism team from the 1970s.

Well, at least that was taken care of.

My friends and I split up after lunch, and the rest of the day flew by. Before I knew it, there we all were at the tryouts.

Jenna admitted she'd been inspired by the Dear Know-It-All letter, and even though she didn't have a leotard, she'd borrowed one and just gone for it. Kristen had screwed up her courage and gone for it too.

I did great on the bars, if I do say so myself, and not too badly on the vault and the trampoline. But my beam and floor exercises were not great. I fell during both, and all I could do was gracefully manage to keep a smile on my face. At least I didn't get hurt.

At the end, we waited while the scores were tallied, and Allie gave me an encouraging pat on the back.

"Either way, I'm proud of you for trying out," she said. And I could tell she really meant it.

"Me too," said Hailey. "Maybe now you'll try out for soccer next year."

"Uh, yeah. Not happening," I said as I nervously awaited the results.

When Coach Lunetta came out to read the list

of names for the next round (they were to come back Saturday morning), my stomach clenched in nervousness. But my name wasn't on the list. Neither was Jenna's. But Kristen's was!

Jenna and I squealed and made a big deal out of Kristen's callback. She actually got kind of teary and bummed we wouldn't be there, but we said she had to make the team now, for all of us.

Jenna said she didn't mind not making it, since it wasn't like she'd trained at all. I had wanted to make it, but I decided that my victory was actually in writing a response that had convinced two people (and who knows, maybe there were others!) to try out, when they otherwise might not have. Seeing as how writing was really where my future lay and, to be fair, where I'd put most of my energy in life, it was its own kind of triumph.

Walking home, I told Allie I was bummed, but I'd live.

Allie was quiet and then she said, "You know, I wanted you to make it, I really did, but a tiny part of me didn't. I'm so sorry."

"Thanks a lot!" I said indignantly.

"It's just . . . it would be torture to have a little sister who's amazing at everything, you know?"

"What?" I was shocked. "But that's how I feel about you!" I accused.

"No, look, I have to slave over every paper, and you write like a dream. It comes so easily for you. You're so organized. You can surf the Web like nobody's business—you know exactly what websites to go to for whatever information you need. Plus, you never worry about makeup or your hair, and you don't need to, either. You always look cute. You're a natural beauty, while I stress out for hours about how I look."

Whoa! Talk about things not really being what they seem!

"Well, I feel the same way about you, so there. Maybe it's just the nature of sisters. Now let's go eat some cinnamon buns!" I laughed and so did Allie, which relieved the seriousness of the discussion, but it left me with a lot to think about.

Journalist Rocked by Sister's Secrets!

My other triumph came later that night, when Michael Lawrence IM'd me to see how the tryouts had gone. I hated admitting I'd failed, but what could I do?

Didn't make it. Total loser.

But then I erased the "Total loser" part. No point in criticizing myself in front of someone I liked. He typed back:

You'll always be a star to me, Pasty.

And with that one little line, I decided all the practice had been worth it.

EXTRA! EXTRA!

Want the scoop on what Samantha is up to next?

Here's a sneak peek of the fifth book in the Dear Know-It-All series:

Everyone's a Critic

Chapter 1

NEWSPAPER STAFF PLAYS MUSICAL CHAIRS. EVERYONE LOSES!

★ ★ ★

Have you ever wished you knew everything? My name is Samantha Martone and I'll tell you a little secret. I'm supposed know everything, at least once a week.

It's a little funny that I write a column for my middle school newspaper, the *Cherry Valley Voice*, called Dear Know-It-All, where I'm supposed to act like I know everything, which I don't.

Here's another secret: I can't tell anyone I write the column—not my annoying older sister, Allie, who's always getting into my business, and not even my BFF, Hailey Jones. But those are the rules, and I've got to stick to them.

Today I was having one of those days—you know those days when nothing goes right?

While I was rushing to make the Voice meeting, I tripped on some invisible bump in the floor and my notebook, where I keep all my lists and notes for the paper, came flying out of my bag. I knelt down to pick it up and two sneakered feet stopped before me.

"Hey, Trippy! Need a hand?" Ah, another nickname—just what I needed. Michael Lawrence is always coming up with ridiculous new nicknames for me. "Pet names," as Hailey calls them. Maybe they were, but they just felt annoying most of the time, especially right now. I looked up and there he was, flashing his baby blues at me, holding out a hand. He must have seen me trip, and it's not the first time he's witnessed my klutziness. My cheeks went hot. How come I always trip in front of Michael?

"That's okay, Mikey." I got up and dusted myself off. "They really should fix that!" I said, glaring at the spot on the floor where I'd tripped. Michael looked where I was looking.

"Yeah, you really gotta watch out for those dangerous flat floors," he said with a grin. "You okay?"

"Just fine, let's go. We're late," I said, trying to ignore the cute smirk on his face. We rushed off and burst into the newsroom. It was full and we had to stand in the back, which is why I'm usually always early.

"It's a tad loud in here. Listen up, fellow journos!" bellowed Mr. Trigg, clapping his hands. The room quieted down.

"Okay, the *Voice* is doing great this year, but we don't want to get stale. Writers must stay on their toes to keep it fresh. That's why we're all going to stretch our comfort zones for this issue and do a little switcheroo."

Now you could hear a pin drop. Michael nudged me and raised his eyebrows. I just shrugged.

"So for the next few issues, the news reporters are going to covers arts, the sportswriters are going to tackle the news, and the arts reporters are going to do sports. Clear?"

Arts? Is he serious? I mean, I love plays and movies and books and all that. But what really gets me excited about writing for the paper is getting the unexpected story. No offense to the arts reporters, but writing a theater review isn't very exciting. Then a headline popped into my head, as they often do: ***Newspaper Staff Plays Musical Chairs. Everyone Loses.***

If you like **DEAR** KNOW-IT-ALL

books, then you'll love

SARANORMAL

Available at your favorite store

Published by Simon Spotlight • KIDS.SimonandSchuster.com